HERE'S TO YOU, RACHEL ROBINSON

HERE'S TO YOU, RACHEL ROBINSON

JUDY BLUME

A Yearling Book

Published by
Bantam Doubleday Dell Books for Young Readers
a division of
Bantam Doubleday Dell Publishing Group, Inc.
1540 Broadway
New York, New York 10036

ISBN: 0-440-40946-2

Reprinted by arrangement with Judy Blume and Orchard Books, a division of Franklin Watts, Inc.

Printed in the United States of America

October 1994

10 9 8 7 6 5 4 3 2 1

OPM

To Amanda

HERE'S TO YOU, RACHEL ROBINSON

ONE

Trouble in our family is spelled with a capital *C* and has been as long as I can remember. The *C* stands for Charles. He's my older brother, two years and four months older to be exact. Ever since the phone call about him last night, I've felt incredibly tense. And now, at this very minute, my parents are driving up to Vermont, to Charles's boarding school, to find out if he's actually been kicked out or if he's just been suspended again.

I tried to take a deep breath. I read an article about relieving tensions in *Psychology Today*. You take a deep breath, then count to ten as you slowly release it. But as I inhaled, I caught the scent of the fresh lilacs on Ms. Lefferts's desk and I started to cough. Ms. Lefferts, my seventh-grade English teacher, looked over at me. She was discussing the three most important elements in making a biography come alive for the reader. When I coughed again, she crossed the room and opened two windows from the bottom, letting in the spring breeze.

· The class was restless, shifting around in their seats, counting the hours till school let out so they could enjoy the first really warm day of the year. But the clock on the wall read 10:17. The day was just beginning. And the date on the chalkboard said FRIDAY, MAY 8. Still seven weeks of school to go.

I forced my mind back to class.

"So now that we've come to the end of our unit on biographies," Ms. Lefferts was saying, "I have an assignment for you." She walked back to her desk and stood there, looking at us, a half smile on her face. She knows exactly how to get our attention. She makes good use of pregnant pauses. I once used that expression in class and have been paying for it ever since. Now I would know better. Now I would say *dramatic* pauses.

"I want you to write a biography of your own lives," Ms. Lefferts continued. "Not an *autobiography*, but a biography. Who can explain the difference?" She took a hair clip out of her desk drawer and held it between her teeth while she gathered her streaked blond hair into a ponytail. She looked around the room as she fastened it, waiting for someone to respond to her question.

Max Wilson raised his hand.

"Yes, Max?" Ms. Lefferts said.

"An autobiography is about the life of a car," Max said.

The class cracked up. Ms. Lefferts didn't.

"Get it?" Max asked. "Auto . . . biography."

"Yes, Max . . . I get it," Ms. Lefferts said. Then she sighed deeply.

I cannot believe that just a few months ago I liked Max Wilson. I actually spent the entire seventh-grade dance with my head nestled on his shoulder. We even kissed in the parking lot while we were waiting for our rides home. What a revolting thought! Now I understand that I never really liked Max, the person. It's just that he is the only boy in seventh grade who's taller than me.

"Rachel . . ." Ms. Lefferts said.

I snapped to attention. Ms. Lefferts was calling on me even though I hadn't raised my hand. I hate when teachers do that. But I said, "The difference between a biography and an autobiography is that in an autobiography the writer is writing about his or her own life. In a biography the writer is writing about the life of someone else."

"Exactly," Ms. Lefferts said. "Thank you, Rachel." Then she went on to explain that she wants us to write a short biography of our own lives, as if we don't know anything about ourselves until we go to the library to do research. "And try to hold it to five pages, please."

Ms. Lefferts never says a paper *has* to be at least five pages. She uses reverse psychology on us. And it always works.

I began to think about my biography right away. Luckily my French teacher was absent, and the substitute told us since she doesn't know one word of French, we could use the period as a study hour. I opened my notebook and started writing, ignoring the kids who were using the period to torture the substitute.

RACHEL LOWILLA ROBINSON
A Biography
Part One—The Unexpected Visitor

Rachel Lowilla Robinson was born tall. The average infant measures nineteen inches at birth but Rachel measured twenty-three. She was the third child born to Nell and Victor Robinson, following Jessica, who was four, and Charles, who was twenty-eight months. The Robinsons had planned on only two children, so Rachel was, as they sometimes put it, the unexpected visitor.

From her mother, Rachel inherited her height and her curly auburn hair. From her father, dark eyes and a love of music. Although her mother was from Boston and her father from Brooklyn, the Robinsons settled in Connecticut to raise their family, in an area of cluster housing called Palfrey's Pond, located just one hour from New York City by train.

Nell Robinson liked to say Rachel was mature from the day she was born. "She was born thirty-five," Mrs. Robinson joked with her friends. But obviously that wasn't true. Rachel was born a baby, like everyone else. She just did things a little earlier. For example, at eight months Rachel was walking. At eighteen months she was speaking in three-word sentences. She could read at three and at four she could pick out tunes on the piano. Her favorite was the theme from "Sesame Street," which Jessica and Charles watched on TV every day. Rachel's first memory was of Charles biting her on the leg, right above her knee. She was barely two at the time.

By first grade it occurred to Rachel that she was different. As her classmates were learning to read, she was finishing the Beverly Cleary books and starting the *Little House* set. As they were learning to add and subtract simple numbers, she enjoyed adding up long columns of figures, especially the register tape from the supermarket. This difference did not make her happy.

I was careful, in Part One, not to tell too much. I told just enough to show Ms. Lefferts I've given serious thought to this assignment. And even though I tried to use interesting details, little-known facts and humorous anecdotes—the three most important elements in making a biography come alive for the reader—I was not about to share the private details of my family life. I was not about to discuss Charles.

The bell rang before I had the chance to start Part Two. I didn't notice until then that I hadn't had any trouble breathing while I was writing. I guess *Psychology Today* is right when they tell you to get your mind off whatever is making you feel tense and onto something else. I picked up my books and went to the cafeteria to meet Stephanie and Alison for lunch.

"What's wrong?" Steph asked, the second I sat down. She was already halfway through a bologna sandwich.

"What do you mean?" I said.

"You're doing that *thing* with your mouth."

"I am?" Last year the dentist made me a kind of retainer to wear at night, to keep me from clenching my jaw, but I left it at Steph's in January and haven't seen it since. My parents still don't know I lost it.

"You get an A *minus* or something?"

"No," I told her.

"Then what?"

"Charles."

"Again?"

I nodded and began to peel a hard-boiled egg. All three of us bring our lunch. We're convinced we'll live longer that way.

"Why doesn't Charles ever come home?" Alison asked, chewing on a carrot stick. She's small and delicate and eats so slowly she hardly ever has time to finish her lunch. But that doesn't bother her. Hardly anything does. She's probably never had trouble breathing in her entire life. She's probably never even felt tense. We are total opposites, so it's amazing that we're friends. "I mean, doesn't he *want* to?" she continued.

"I guess not." I salted my egg, then bit into it.

"I don't get it," Alison said. She's never met Charles, since he left for Vermont last August and she didn't move here from L.A. until Labor Day. Actually Steph met Alison first and they hit it off right away. She didn't even tell me Alison's adopted or that her birth mother's Vietnamese until school started. I used to worry that Steph, who's been my best friend since second grade, would forget about me. Actually, I still do. But at the moment it seems to be working out okay, even though I know she and Alison prefer each other's company to mine.

"There's nothing to get," I told her. "Except that he's impossible! Now, could we please change the subject?"

"Impossible how?" Alison asked, ignoring my request.

"Rude and obnoxious."

Alison looked over at Stephanie to see if she agreed. Stephanie nodded. "He's definitely rude." Steph took a mirror out of her backpack and set it on the table. She opened her mouth wide to make sure food wasn't caught in her braces. Stephanie is the least self-conscious person I know.

"How'd he get that way?" Alison asked.

I was really getting annoyed and Alison could tell. She offered me her bag of potato chips. "How does anybody get that way?" I said, reaching in and grabbing a handful.

TWO

When I got home from school, my cousin Tarren was at the house. She's twenty-two and has a ten-month-old baby, Roddy. She could tell I was surprised to see her. "Nell and Victor had to go to Vermont," she said, using my parents' first names. "It has something to do with Charles," she added, as if I didn't know.

"Jess and I could have managed on our own," I told her, irritated that Mom had asked her to come over without discussing it with me.

Tarren bent down to tie her running shoes. She's tall, like all the women in our family, but her hair is black and her eyes blue. Jessica and I were bridesmaids at her wedding two years ago. Now she's divorced. She and Bill, the guy she married, didn't get along even though they went together all through high school and two years of college. Tarren says Bill couldn't accept adult responsibilities, like being a father. He moved out west after the divorce and spends all his time hang gliding. His picture was on the cover of *Hang Glider* magazine a few months ago. He looked like some sort of strange prehistoric bird.

"Nell asked me to spend the night," Tarren said, "since tonight is Jessica's junior prom and all. . . ."

I had totally forgotten about Jessica's prom. I'd be devastated if it were my junior prom and Mom and Dad were away because of Charles.

"I promised we'd take lots of pictures," Tarren said. "I brought my new camera." She grabbed it off the kitchen counter. "It's a PHD. The guy at the store claims you can't take a bad picture with it." She pointed it at me. "You know what PHD stands for?" she asked. *"Press Here, Dummy!"* She laughed as she pressed but I jumped out of the way.

"Rachel! That was my last shot."

"Sorry."

"I guess it doesn't matter. Nell said you've got two rolls of film in the fridge."

I couldn't believe that in the midst of a family crisis Mom would remember we had film in the refrigerator. I guess Tarren could tell what I was thinking because she said, "Nell is the most amazing woman!"

I've heard that expression more times than I can count. It's true Mom is a successful trial lawyer, but

I don't see what's so amazing about that. I expect to do just as much with my life.

"Between you and me," Tarren continued, "I think it's grossly unfair that Nell has to spend so much of her time worrying about your brother. A lot of kids would jump at the chance to change places with him. He doesn't appreciate what he has. That's his problem!"

I didn't feel like talking about Charles, so I told Tarren I had homework and went up to my room.

Later the two of us had supper in the kitchen while Jessica soaked in a bubble bath upstairs. Tarren likes to hear about school since she's studying to be a teacher. So I told her about the biography and what Max Wilson had said in class. She laughed and laughed. She'll probably be a good teacher. She wants to teach fourth grade, which should be just right for her. We ate standing at the counter—tuna right from the can, lettuce leaves pulled off the head and, for dessert, frozen Milky Ways left over from Halloween. We're lucky we didn't break our teeth on them.

"Is this how you eat every night?" I asked, thinking of the way we sit down to dinner, the table set with place mats and pretty dishes.

"Rachel," Tarren said, "when you have a ten-month-old to worry about, *plus* papers and exams, you just don't have time to think about meals. If my mom doesn't fix supper, I'm happy grazing. When Roddy's older, it'll be different. I'll have a teaching job and my own place and . . ." Her voice drifted off for a minute. "But not everyone can be a wonder woman like your mother."

"Dad helps. He does all the grocery shopping."

"Well, I'm a single parent. There won't be anyone around to help me."

"Maybe you'll get married again," I suggested, causing Tarren to choke on her Natural Lime Spritzer, which she was swigging straight out of the bottle.

"Pul-eeese . . ." she said, wiping her mouth with the back of her hand. She sounded exactly like one of my friends.

We could hear Jessica rustling in her magenta taffeta prom dress before we actually saw her. She let me try it on last week. It fit perfectly. Jess and I could be doubles except she has a major case of acne. She uses a heavy medicated makeup that hides some of it on good days. On bad days nothing can hide it.

As Jess came down the stairs, Tarren snapped away. I was surprised when Jess posed for the camera. Usually she refuses to have her picture taken. But tonight she put her arms around me, as if I were her date, and twirled me across the room until we were both laughing our heads off and so dizzy we fell back onto the sofa.

"You two are so great!" Tarren said. "You remind me

of me and my friends when we were your age." She turned serious. "Enjoy it now," she told us, "because life isn't always all you thought it'd be." She paused for a minute, then added, "I speak from experience."

Neither of us knew how to respond. Finally Jessica cleared her throat and said, "Tarren . . . didn't you say you have to run over to the library?"

"Well . . . yes," Tarren answered, "but only for a little while."

"Why don't you go now?" Jess suggested. "The library closes at nine."

I found it strange that Jessica was suddenly so anxious for Tarren to go to the library.

"I've just got to pick up some books," Tarren explained to me. "We're studying the gifted and talented child this month."

I felt my face turn hot.

"I won't be long," she said.

As soon as she was gone, Jessica let out a sigh and raced upstairs. Ten minutes later she returned transformed in Mom's slinky black dress, satin heels and dangling earrings. She'd put on dark, wine-colored lipstick and had pinned her hair back on one side, letting the rest fall over her face.

I almost passed out. "Jessica . . ."

She held up her hand. "Don't say it, Rachel. We'll have pictures of me in pink."

"But Mom will—" I began again.

"Mom's not here, is she? And if someone at school tells Dad, it will be too late. The prom will be over."

Dad teaches history at the high school and coaches the track team. Someone will definitely tell him about this. Someone will say, "That was some outfit your daughter wore to the prom, Victor!"

A car horn tooted. Jess took a quick look out the window. "My chariot," she said.

I followed as she ran down the front walk. "And not a word about this to anyone," she called over her shoulder, tripping on Mom's heels. "Understand?"

Her friends Richie, Ed, Marcy and Kristen whooped and whistled when they saw her. Jess says she has the best friends ever. She says she can tell them anything. But I think they were surprised tonight.

"Get the camera, Rachel," Jess called. I ran inside for Tarren's PHD and snapped one group photo before they all piled back into the car.

I tried to imagine the three of us—Stephanie, Alison and me—going to our junior prom four years from now. Will we go in a group like Jess and her friends, or with individual dates? Jess says it's better to go in a group. There are fewer disappointments that way. I don't know. I think it would be more romantic to go with someone you really like. But if it came down to Max Wilson or my friends, I would definitely choose my friends.

As they pulled out, I called, "Drive carefully!"

"We always do," Jess called back, laughing.

I watched them drive away. Then I went back into the house, wondering what Mom will say if she finds out Jess wore her black dress. *She'll probably blame herself,* I thought. *She'll probably say Jess is* acting out.

THREE

Acting out is exactly the expression Dr. Sparks used to describe Charles's behavior. He's the psychologist who evaluated him last year, the one who suggested he go away to school.

I admit it was a great relief when Charles left for Vermont last August—even though boarding school is a luxury we can't really afford, not with three kids who will soon be ready for college. I know my parents sometimes feel guilty about the decision to send him away to school. But I don't. Now I can invite my friends over without worrying.

I never told anyone I'd read Dr. Sparks's report. I'd found it by chance on the dining room table, mixed in with Mom's legal pads and reference books, while I was searching for a letter from music camp. It said Charles was *acting out* as a way of getting the attention he craved. Well, I could have told my parents that for free!

Thinking about Charles made me feel weak, so I took the last piece of watermelon out of the refrigerator and sat at the kitchen table slurping it up while I waited for Tarren to return from the library. When I finished, I collected the seeds and stood halfway across the kitchen. Then, one by one, I tried spitting them into the sink. Stephanie had a party on the last day of school last year and spitting watermelon seeds from a distance was one of the games we played. I was hopeless, missing the target every time. Even though I think it's incredibly stupid, I've been practicing in secret ever since. Tonight I hit my target eight out of eleven times.

The watermelon reminded me of dinner last night. We'd sat down to eat early, as soon as Mom had walked in, because Jess was in a hurry to get back to school. She and Ed were on the decorating committee for the prom. They were transforming the gym into some kind of futuristic fantasy with a hundred silver balloons and yards and yards of tinsel.

We'd been talking about the prom all through dinner, but just as we were finishing the watermelon Mom said, "Guess who's on the governor's short list for Superior Court?"

I had no idea what she was talking about, but Dad pushed back his chair, practically leaped across the table and lifted Mom out of her seat. "I've always wanted to make it with a judge," he said.

They kissed, then Mom told him, "You'll have to wait till the end of the month to find out."

"Find out what?" I asked.

"I've been nominated for a judgeship," Mom said.

"A judge?" Jessica asked. "You're going to be a judge?"

"Maybe," Mom said.

"What would that mean?" I asked. "Would you have to quit your job at the firm?"

"Yes," Mom said. "Being a judge is a full-time job."

"I can't imagine you as a judge," Jess said.

"I can," I told her. "Mom would make an excellent judge."

"I didn't say she wouldn't," Jess said.

"Would you get murder cases?" I asked Mom.

"That would depend on which court I'm assigned to," she said. "If it's criminal court, I could get murder cases. If it's domestic court, I'd get divorces and child custody cases, and if it's civil court . . ." She paused. "But it's too soon to think about the details. First we have to see if I'm actually appointed."

My mind was racing. What if Mom gets criminal court and sends a murderer to jail and he escapes and finds out where we live and comes after her. . . . I'd read about a case like that in the paper. Maybe we'll have bodyguards to protect us like the President. Not that I want to live with bodyguards. And I certainly don't want to be escorted to school every day. I don't think that would go over very well with my friends. Probably they won't want to come to my house if that happens. Probably their parents won't even let them!

Jessica brought me back from my *what ifs* when she jumped up from the table. "I'm going to be late! Be home around ten," she called as the screen door slammed.

Mom flinched. She hates it when the door slams.

It was my night to help clean up the kitchen. Mom makes out lists every Sunday night—household jobs, groceries, errands, appointments. Steph is envious of the chalkboard in our kitchen with the dinner menu printed on it every day. She never knows what's for dinner until her mother gets home from work with some kind of takeout. If it were up to Dad and Jess, our household would be chaotic. But Mom says if you're organized, everything in life is easier. I agree. Except maybe dealing with Charles.

I started clearing the plates off the table. When the phone rang, I ran for it, sure it was Stephanie or Alison. I wouldn't tell them anything about Mom being a judge yet. I'd wait until it was definite.

But it wasn't Alison or Steph. It was Timothy Norton, the director of the Dorrance School. I put my hand over the receiver and whispered to Mom and Dad, "It's about Charles."

Dad turned off the water at the sink and dried his hands on his jeans. I held the phone out to him as Mom raced upstairs to pick up the extension in their room. I felt my dinner sloshing around in my stomach. Yet from the tone of Dad's voice, I didn't think it was as serious as last time, when Mr. Norton called to tell us about Charles's accident.

That was last January, right after the holidays. Charles had gone for a joyride on his teacher's Yamaha. It was a wet night and he'd lost control, skidding across the road and crashing into a tree. He'd wound up with cuts and bruises plus a gash in his leg requiring twelve stitches.

Still, they said he was lucky because he hadn't been wearing a helmet and he could have been killed. I am somewhat ashamed to admit this, but at the time I'd let that thought run through my mind. *He could have been killed.* Then I'd pushed it away. I don't want Charles to die. Dying is too final. My parents would blame themselves and never get over it. Besides, he's my brother. I'm supposed to care about him. Even though the teacher didn't press charges, Charles was suspended for a week. But he didn't come home. He went to Aunt Joan's house in New Hampshire, instead.

A minute after Dad hung up the phone, Mom came back into the kitchen. She'd aged ten years in ten minutes. She thinks she's good at hiding her feelings because she doesn't talk about them. But she can't fool me. I can read her thoughts by the changes in her face. The crease in her forehead was deeper, her mouth was stiff and her shoulders hunched.

Dad put an arm around her. She gave him a pained look.

"What?" I asked.

Mom didn't answer.

"What?" I said again, this time to Dad.

"He hasn't handed in his papers and he refuses to take any exams," Dad explained. Then he went back to the sink, turned the water on full blast and began to scour the lasagna pan as if his life depended on it.

"What does that mean?" I asked Mom. "Will he have to do ninth grade a third time?"

"Absolutely not!" Mom said, pulling herself together. She stood tall and erect and looked me straight in the eye. "And he *didn't* repeat ninth grade. The system at Dorrance is different from public school. You know that. It was in Charles's best interest to start over as a freshman."

Mom marched across the kitchen and started loading the dishwasher, with all the dishes facing the same direction. She can't stand how Dad does it, shoving things in any which way.

"He's always been too young for his class, emotionally," Mom continued, building her case as if she were in court. She's full of excuses when it comes to Charles.

"And I don't want you to discuss this with anyone, Rachel."

"Mom!" I was annoyed that she thought I needed reminding.

"We should have held him back a year before first grade," Mom said, drumming the counter with her fingertips, "but who knew then?"

"Nell . . ." Dad said. "Rachel doesn't need to worry about this."

They looked at each other for a minute. Then Mom said, "You're right." But she kept drumming the counter. It was amazing how one phone call about Charles could change everything.

"This doesn't mean he's coming home, does it?" I asked. My mouth felt dry, as if I couldn't swallow.

"We won't know until we meet with Mr. Norton at Dorrance," Dad said.

"You'd better call for a substitute," Mom told Dad. "And I'll have to cancel my deposition." She opened a kitchen drawer, pulled out a pad and pencil and began to make a list. Without even looking up, she said, "Let the cats in, would you, Rachel. They're scratching at the screen."

I held the screen door for Burt and Harry, then bolted from the room with them at my heels. I raced up the stairs and locked myself into my room, throwing open all the windows. The night air smelled like summer. I wished it really *were* summer. I wished I could go to music camp tomorrow. Then I wouldn't have to think about Charles or what might happen if he came home.

I took my flute out of its case, sat at my music stand and began to play a Handel sonata. Music takes me someplace else. To a world where I feel safe and happy. Sometimes I make mistakes but I can fix them. Sometimes I don't get exactly the sound I want, but I can find it if I keep trying. With music it's up to me. With music I'm in control.

FOUR

ell me more about Charles," Alison said.

It was Saturday morning and the three of us—Stephanie, Alison and me—were walking along the water's edge at the town beach. It's not an ocean beach. It's on the Sound. In fourth grade we had to memorize the difference between a sound and a bay. It's funny how you remember things like that.

The weather was still balmy but more humid than yesterday, and we wore shorts and T-shirts for the first time since last September. A few people on the beach were in bathing suits, working on an early tan. I hate baking in the sun. My skin gets freckled, my eyes sting and sometimes I get sneezing fits.

I've decided Alison's fascination with my brother has to do with the fact that until now she's been the only child in her family. Actually she's still the only child. Her mother is pregnant but the baby isn't due until July.

"Well, for one thing, Charles has a great sense of humor," Steph told Alison. "That is, when he wants to." She paused for a minute. "And he's extremely cute."

"Really?" Alison asked me. "I didn't know he was cute."

"I refuse to participate in this conversation!" I told them both.

Maizie, Alison's small, furry-faced dog, was digging up a bone buried in the sand. When we first met Alison, she told us her dog could talk and Stephanie believed her. Steph is incredibly gullible. She believes anything you tell her. She even believed her father was away on a business trip when it was painfully obvious to the rest of us her parents had separated.

Alison turned to Steph. "If Charles comes home from boarding school, will he finish ninth grade at Fox?" She acted as if Steph had all the answers. I never should have told them my parents went to Vermont. I never should have told them anything. My mother was right. This is family business. You can't expect anyone else to understand.

"Maybe he'll be in Jeremy Dragon's class," Alison said to Steph. I loved the way they were carrying on this conversation as if I weren't there.

"Oh, that'd be perfect!" Stephanie said, jabbing me in the side. "Right, Rachel?"

"I find that a totally revolting idea!" I said. Jeremy Dragon is our name for the best-looking boy in ninth grade. He wears a chartreuse satin team jacket with a black dragon on the back. I'm the only seventh grader in his math class.

"But it *is* possible," Alison said.

"Anything's possible!" I admitted. My mind was filling with *what ifs*. What if Charles comes home today? What if he *does* have to do ninth grade again, and at *my* junior high? What if he makes friends with Jeremy Dragon and Jeremy Dragon starts hanging out at our house and Charles humiliates me in front of him and my parents won't listen and . . .

"Rachel . . ." Stephanie sang, waving a hand in front of my face. "Where are you?"

I don't know why but as soon as Stephanie said that, I took off. I ran as fast as I could, with Maizie at my heels, barking.

I could hear Alison and Stephanie laughing and shouting, "Rachel . . . what are you doing? Rachel . . . wait! Ra . . . chel!"

There was no way they could catch me. My legs are twice as long as Alison's. And Steph isn't fast enough. Only Maizie could keep up with me. I kept running, from one end of the beach to the other. Finally I collapsed on the sand, totally out of breath, with a stitch in my side.

We went to Alison's house for lunch. Leon, her stepfather, made us grilled cheese and tomato sandwiches.

Alison's mother, Gena Farrell, was at the counter squeezing lemons. Suddenly she put her hands on her belly and said, "Ooh . . . Matthew's playing soccer this morning." Gena is a famous TV actress with her own series. But at home she acts like a regular parent. Alison says her pregnancy is a surprise to everyone since she's forty years old and the doctors told her long ago she'd never be able to have biological children. That's why she adopted Alison.

"Let me feel," Leon said. He put his hands on Gena's belly. "Good going, Matthew. That's a goal!"

They talk about the baby as if he were already born. Gena's had tests to make sure he's okay. That's how they know it's a boy. His full name will be Matthew Farrell Wishnik.

Before we finished lunch there was a rumble of thunder. Maizie whimpered and hid under the table. After lunch, while the rain poured down, the three of us watched a movie. Alison's family has a great collection of tapes. By the time it was over, it was close to four and the rain had stopped. I looked out the window and saw Dad's Explorer parked outside our house.

"I have to go," I said.

"Promise to call right away and tell us what's happening," Alison said.

But I wasn't making any promises.

FIVE

he front door to our house was open. I called hello but no one answered. I ran upstairs, looking for Mom or Dad. Instead I found my worst fears coming true. Charles was in my room, at my desk!

I stood in my doorway, frozen. For just a minute I saw Charles the way Steph does—as a boy with dark hair, dreamy hazel eyes and a scar on his forehead. The scar makes him look interesting, not just handsome. Suddenly Grandpa Robinson's voice popped into my head. "Too bad the boy got all the looks in your family, Victor," he once told Dad. I was incredibly hurt when he said that, even though I was only eight.

Charles began to read aloud from my biography. "Rachel is credited with having discovered the vaccine, now widely used, to prevent hair balls in lions."

"Put that down!" My heart was pounding but I spoke slowly and quietly.

"Hair balls in lions?" Charles asked, acknowledging my presence. He didn't seem concerned that I'd caught him red-handed. "Hair balls in lions?" he repeated, laughing.

"I *said* put that down!" I sounded just like my mother when she turns on her lawyer voice. But that wasn't enough to stop Charles. He kept right on reading from Part Two of my biography, the part I call "Rachel, The Later Years." I'd handwritten it on one of Mom's legal pads early this morning. I'd enjoyed inventing my three brilliant careers—first as a veterinarian doing research on large cats in Africa, then as a musician with the New York Philharmonic, and finally as a great stage actress specializing in Shakespeare. I'd also given myself a husband and two children, all wildly successful.

"Her son, Toledo . . ." Charles paused, looking at me. "You named your son for a town in Ohio?"

"Spain, you idiot!" I tore across the room and reached for my biography. "Toledo, Spain!" I'm taller than Charles, but he's fast and he held the pages high above his head. Every time I grabbed for them, he'd transfer them to his other hand and dance around the room.

I felt so desperate I kicked, catching him on the shin. Then I dug my nails into his arm. I've never had a physical fight in my entire life. But I would have kept it up if he hadn't yelled, "Cut it out, Rachel . . .

or kiss your biography good-bye." He had both hands on my paper now, ready to rip it in half.

I didn't doubt that he'd do it. And there was no other copy. Even though I'd meant to enter it in my computer, I'd been rushing to meet Stephanie and Alison and figured I'd do it later. Tears stung my eyes but I would never cry in front of him. I would never give him that satisfaction!

I backed away and stood at the foot of my bed, my hands grasping the white iron rail. "You mess that up and you're dead!" I told him.

"Then you'll have to rewrite your biography," he said. "At thirteen Rachel Lowilla Robinson murdered her brother, Charles. She spent the rest of her life in jail. All eighty-four years of it."

"No," I said. "It would go more like, Since the judge and jury agreed that her brother provoked her, Rachel was acquitted and lived happily ever after."

"You won't get off that easy," he said. "They'll get you for manslaughter, at the very least."

"I'm a juvenile," I told him. "At the most I'll get probation."

"I wouldn't count on that."

"Really," I said. "Well, let's go and ask Mom, since she's just been nominated as a judge."

I could tell by the expression on his face I'd caught him by surprise. *Good!* He laid my biography on the desk. "Isn't that something!" he said. "Another milestone for our extraordinary family." He flopped in my favorite chair and draped his legs over the arm. "So . . . are you surprised to see me, little sister?"

"I'm never surprised by you," I said, which was a big lie. His moods can switch so fast you never know what to expect, which is the single worst thing about him. "When are you going back to school?" I asked, trying to sound as if I didn't care. "Or were you actually kicked out this time?"

"Expelled, Rachel. The expression is *expelled*."

"Were you *expelled* on purpose?" I asked, wondering what exactly this would mean.

"Yeah. I missed you so much I couldn't wait to come home." He inspected his arm where I'd dug in my nails. He could have smashed me. But that's not Charles's style. Instead he gave me his best, dimpled smile. "You've done a real job on your room. What color do you call this?"

"Peach," I answered.

"Peach," he repeated, looking around. "Maybe I'll switch rooms with you. This one is bigger than mine. And since I'm older, I should have the bigger room, don't you think?"

Was he serious? I couldn't tell. This *used* to be his room. When we were younger, Jess and I shared her room. But then Charles campaigned for the small room on the first floor, and when Mom and Dad finally agreed, I got this one.

Aunt Joan sent my bed and the wicker furniture from her antique shop in New Hampshire. And Tarren gave me the rag rug for my birthday. I'm not about to give up my room! But Mom and Dad wouldn't ask me to, would they?

Now I felt totally confused, the way I always do around him. I wanted to scream, *Go back to school! Go anywhere! But leave us alone!* Except in our family we don't scream. We swallow hard, instead.

Charles stood up and stretched. "I think I'll go down and unpack. My room has several advantages over yours. . . ." He walked in front of the bed, where I was sitting. He put his face close to mine and I could smell onions on his breath.

"Besides," he said, "if I had to sleep in a room with peach walls, I'd puke." He made a disgusting retching sound, and as I jumped back, he laughed.

When he was gone, I closed the bedroom door, lay down on my bed and cried.

Mom and Dad tried to make Charles's first supper at home a festive occasion, even though being expelled from school isn't normally an event to celebrate. Charles came to the table wearing a T-shirt that said I DON'T NEED YOUR ATTITUDE . . . I HAVE MY OWN. None of us commented. Dad grilled chicken with mustard sauce and Mom made Charles's favorite coleslaw, so full of vinegar it choked me. But Charles loved it. The sour taste agreed with him.

In the middle of dinner he said, "So I think I'll drop out for a while . . . maybe get a job or something."

"That's not an option," Dad said.

"You have to be sixteen to drop out, don't you?" I asked. "And your birthday's not until November."

"Aha . . ." Charles said. "The child prodigy speaks."

I hate it when he calls me that. It makes me feel as if I've done something wrong, something to be ashamed of.

"It's just a matter of finding the right school," Mom said to Charles softly.

Charles exploded. "There is no right school for me! Don't you get it by now? I'm allergic to school!"

"Excuse me," Jessica said. "I've got to pick up my prom pictures before Fotomat closes."

"Excuse me, too," I said, shoving back my chair. "I have a ton of homework."

Charles shook his head. "Those daughters of yours need to be taught some manners," he told Mom and Dad. "They shouldn't be allowed to leave the table when the rest of us are still eating. If I didn't know better, I'd think it has something to do with me. I'd think they're not really as glad to see me as they pretend."

"They might be if it wasn't for your attitude," Mom said.

"Attitude?" Charles said, looking down at his T-shirt. "If we're talking attitude here—"

But Mom didn't wait for him to finish. "Just stop it, Charles!"

"Nell . . ." Dad said, quietly. "Let it go."

"Right," Charles said snidely. "Let it go, Mom. We don't want to upset Dad, do we?"

Later, I think we all regretted how badly dinner had gone and we gathered in the living room. "What's this?" Mom asked, examining the red marks on Charles's arm where I'd dug my nails into his skin. They were sitting next to each other on the small sofa.

"Harry," Charles said, using the cat as an excuse.

"I don't like the way it looks," Mom told him. "Put some peroxide on it."

"Yeah . . . yeah . . ."

"I'm serious, Charles. It could get infected."

Charles smiled at me.

Dad perched on the sofa arm, next to Mom, and Jess passed around her prom pictures. As she did, she gave me a private look, letting me know she'd already removed the group shot showing her in Mom's slinky black dress.

"Oh, Jess . . ." Mom said, studying the pictures. "That shade of pink is perfect on you."

"Magenta," I said.

Everyone looked at me.

"Well, it's more magenta than pink, isn't it?" I asked.

"*Magenta*," Charles said, making me wish I'd never heard the word. "Glad to know you're keeping up with your Crayola colors, Rachel."

Before I could think of something to say back, Dad held out one of Jessica's pictures and said, "Brings back memories, doesn't it, Nell?"

Mom said, "In my day you had to be *asked*."

Dad put his arm around Mom's shoulder and nuzzled her. "If they could see you now, those guys would be eating their hearts out."

"Good," Mom said, smiling at him.

Mom isn't beautiful like Alison's mother but she is very *put together*. She wears classic clothes and her hair is always perfect, whether it's loose or tied back. She says grooming is more important than looks. I hope that's true because when Mom was young she was awkward—too tall like me—and had a serious case of acne, like Jess.

"So, Jessica . . ." Charles said, studying one prom picture after the other. "Do they still call you *Pizza Face*, or is it mostly *Jess the Mess*?"

Jessica grabbed the pictures out of his hand. "Asshole," she hissed. "I wish you'd never been born!" She started from the room in tears, then turned back to face him. "And I hope you get the worst zits ever. I hope they swell and ooze and hurt so bad you go to bed crying every night!"

"Thanks, Jess . . ." Charles called, as if Jess had given him a compliment. "I appreciate that."

Mom ran after Jessica, and Dad said, "Dammit, Charles . . . we're a family. Could we please try to act like one?"

"I am trying," Charles said. "It's just that my sisters are so sensitive they can't even take a joke."

SIX

I lay in bed for a long time that night, stroking Burt and Harry, as I listened to Jess crying in her room. I don't understand Charles. I don't understand how he can be so cruel and hateful.

Unfortunately cystic acne runs in our family. Mom and Dad actually met at a drugstore, buying the same medicated skin cream, when they were first-year law students at Columbia. They started going together right away and were married the week they graduated. Mom says Dad is the first person who ever talked to her about acne. Everyone else shied away from the subject. It made them too uncomfortable.

Until then, Mom never even went out with a guy. Looking back, she says her acne was a blessing in disguise. It freed her to concentrate on schoolwork. She won a scholarship to college and another to law school, and she always graduated with honors. But she never kissed a guy until she met Dad and she was twenty-two at the time! I'm glad I've already had my first kiss. Not that I'm proud of having kissed Max Wilson, but at the time it seemed like the right thing to do.

There are a lot of things in life I consider unfair and cystic acne is one of them. I'm not talking about your basic teenage acne. I'm talking about painful lumps and bumps that swell and distort your face. I don't know what I'll do if I get it. Jess has tried antibiotics but they haven't helped much. Mom is always saying, "It cleared up before my thirtieth birthday," as if that will help Jess feel better. Imagine waking up every day with your problem right there on your face for the whole world to see! And having to deal with stupid guys calling you *Pizza Face* and *Jess the Mess*.

I consider Jess one of the bravest people I know. She gets up and goes to school five days a week. She has friends. She even manages to have a sense of humor.

When I finally did fall asleep, I tossed and turned and had bizarre dreams. I woke at dawn, sweaty and anxious, so I crept down to the kitchen and made myself a bowl of Cream of Wheat, with just a drop of brown sugar and milk. Whenever I feel my stomach tying up in knots, I eat comfort food—bananas, mashed potatoes, cooked cereal.

I was thumbing through the Sunday paper and feeling better when Charles waltzed in, humming to

himself. "Good morning, little sister," he sang, as if
we were old friends. "Did you get your beauty
sleep?" He looked at me, then answered his own
question. "I guess not."

I mumbled a few choice words under my breath.

"What was that?" he said.

"Never mind."

He began pulling out baking pans, mixing bowls
and ingredients from the refrigerator.

"What are you doing?" I asked.

"It's Mother's Day, Rachel."

"I *know* it's Mother's Day."

"So . . . I'm going to bake something special for our
dear old mom."

"Since when do you know how to bake?"

He shook his head. "There's so much you don't
know about me."

That was certainly true. I never would have
guessed Charles would remember Mother's Day. I
thought about the gift Jess and I had bought for
her—a subscription to *Metropolitan Home*. Mom's
always saying she needs to redo the living room, if
only she could find the time. We hope this will
encourage her.

I read the rest of the paper while Charles baked. I
have to admit, when he pulled a scrumptious-look-
ing coffee cake out of the oven forty-five minutes
later, I was pretty amazed. He tested it with a tooth-

pick, then set it on a cooling rack. The smell made my mouth water.

I watched as he prepared a steaming pot of coffee, poured a pitcher of orange juice, and arranged it all on a tray. At the last minute he plucked a flower from the bunch on the table and set it on top of his cake. Then he took the Sunday paper, including the section I was reading, folded it up and tucked it under his arm. Before he started out of the room, he looked at me. "Impressed?" he asked.

He knew I was, even though I didn't say a word.

A minute later Jessica came into the kitchen, still in her nightshirt, her hair disheveled, her face covered with dark green goo that smelled faintly of seaweed. She yawned.

"What are you doing up so early?" I asked.

"Couldn't sleep." She opened the refrigerator and stuck her head inside. "I just met our *nightmare* on the stairs."

"He was bringing Mom breakfast in bed . . ." I told her, "in honor of Mother's Day!"

"Oh, God . . ." Jess said from inside the refrigerator. "He's such a hypocrite!"

"Suppose they don't find another school for him?" I asked. "What do you think will happen? I mean, he won't finish ninth grade at Fox, will he?"

"Mom and Dad are smart. They'll figure out something."

"But I've got to know now!"

"There's no way you can know, Rachel. And worrying about it isn't going to help." She backed out of the refrigerator and touched her face to see if the mask had hardened yet. It hadn't.

"Does that mean you think he's going to stay here?" I asked.

"It's his home, isn't it?" she said. "Mom and Dad are his parents, aren't they? They can't just *give* him away."

"Maybe they could send him to live with someone else," I suggested.

"Like who?"

"I don't know . . . Aunt Joan? She took him when he was suspended."

"That was for a week," Jess said. "Don't get your hopes up." She stuck her face back inside the refrigerator.

Mom came downstairs, beaming. "Charles baked a fabulous coffee cake," she said to me. "You've got to try it. It's light and fluffy and the topping's perfect." Then she noticed Jess. "Jessica, please close the refrigerator. Everything will spoil."

Jess touched her cheek. This time she was satisfied. The seaweed mask had set, leaving her with a hardened green face and white circles around her eyes. She looked like a green raccoon.

"Maybe I'll get a job as a baker," Charles said, following Mom into the kitchen.

"That could be a wonderful summer experience for you," Mom said, "if you don't have to go to summer school."

"I wasn't talking about a *summer* job."

"We've already been through that," Mom reminded him. "Let's not spoil our day."

"Oh, right!" He thumped his head with the back of his hand. "Today is Mother's Day . . . a family holiday. I hope my sisters remember that."

"Excuse me," I said. "I'll be in my room, practicing."

"Practicing?" Charles sneered.

"The flute!" I shouted.

"Oh, the flute," he said. "I thought you had something more exciting in mind."

"Grow up, Charles!" Jessica said, following me out of the kitchen.

"I'm trying . . ." he said, "I'm trying. . . ."

"Maybe you need to try harder," Mom told him.

"Push, push, push . . ." Charles said. "That's our family motto."

Mom ignored him and called after us, "Please be ready by eleven, girls. We're going to see Gram then."

Gram is Mom's mother. Her name is Kate Carter Babcock and she's seventy-six. She had a stroke a year ago and has lived at a nursing home ever since.

I get very depressed when we go to visit. *What's the use?* I think. *What's the use of going through a whole lifetime, then winding up like Gram?*

Gram can't talk. The stroke affected the left side of her brain. She makes sounds, not anything we can understand, though. They tried therapy for a while, but when she didn't respond they stopped. I don't know if she understands what we say, or even if she recognizes us. I like to think she does.

Today, when we got there, Gram was dressed for company. The nurse had brushed blush on her cheeks, and it stood out against her pale skin in two uneven circles. She sat in her wheelchair, facing the window that overlooks the garden. She had a soft, pastel-colored blanket across her lap. I recognized it as one of Roddy's baby blankets. When he was born, Tarren received so many she brought half a dozen to the nursing home.

I was glad Gram's chair was turned to the window, because one time we came to visit and someone had left her facing the blank wall. Mom was furious. She'd gone straight to the director to complain.

Mom opened the white florist's box we'd brought and took out a small orchid corsage. She slid it onto Gram's wrist. "Happy Mother's Day," she said, kissing Gram's cheek.

"Happy Mother's Day," Jess and I repeated in unison.

Then Charles stepped forward and kneeled beside Gram's chair. "Hey, Gram . . . remember me . . . your one and only grandson?" He paused for a moment. "So, how's it going?"

Gram turned her head toward Charles. Her eyes seemed to focus on his face. After that it was as if the rest of us didn't exist.

We took Gram for a stroll around the grounds. The tulips and daffodils were in full bloom, and the dogwoods were about to flower. I guess if you have to be in a nursing home, it's better to be in one with pretty gardens.

Mom pushed Gram's wheelchair. Dad hung back. I think visiting Gram reminds him of his own parents, especially his father. After Grandpa Robinson died, when I was in fourth grade, Dad went to bed for six weeks. I was very scared at the time, thinking he was going to die, too. That's when I started running through my *what ifs* at bedtime. My stomach was always tied up in knots. I went to the school nurse every day. Finally my teacher called Mom and asked her to come to school. The next day I was taken to Dr. Klaff for a complete medical checkup. Dr. Klaff said there was nothing physically wrong with me, except that I needed to learn to relax.

Then one day, just as I was getting used to the situation, Dad got out of bed and decided to change his life. He didn't want to be a lawyer anymore. He wanted to be a teacher. So he went back to school to get a degree in education, then got the job teaching history at the high school. We never talk about that time in our lives.

As we walked with Gram, Charles kept up a steady one-way conversation with her. "Yeah, I'm doing really well at this school, Gram. Dorrance . . . that's what it's called. I'm probably going to be class president next year and I've already made the varsity track team. That's how it is with us . . . we always have to be the best! But I guess you know that, Gram. . . . I mean, you're the one who raised Mom, right?"

"Charles . . ." Mom said, warning him.

"Yeah, right . . ." Charles answered.

Gram seemed mesmerized, as if the sound of Charles's voice were enough to make her day. I couldn't help wondering what she was thinking. Did she understand he was feeding her a pack of lies?

An hour later, as we said good-bye to Gram, Charles turned away from her wheelchair with tears in his eyes. When he caught me watching, he walked off by himself.

Gram made a few sounds. Maybe she was calling to him. Who knows? But the nurse had a different interpretation. "We're ready for our dinner, aren't we?" she asked Gram in singsong.

"Will you please not address her in that tone of

voice," Mom said to the nurse. "Will you please talk to her as if she were a healthy person!"

"But she's not, is she?" the nurse replied tartly.

Mom was about to pounce but Dad reminded her this is the best nursing home in the area. There's a waiting list to get in and if Mom makes a fuss again, the director will call, threatening to expel Gram. Wouldn't that be something . . . Charles and Gram expelled in the same week! Mom backed off and headed for the car.

The rest of us followed. Charles walked behind me, deliberately stepping on the backs of my shoes, pulling them off my feet. I thought about sticking out my foot and tripping him, but I didn't feel like making a scene. So I moved away and walked closer to Mom. She put her arm around my shoulders and said, "Don't be sad, honey. Gram's had a long life. And she's not suffering. We should all be grateful for that."

SEVEN

By Monday morning I was seething. And all because of Charles!

So at the bus stop, when Dana Carpenter, a ninth grader who also lives at Palfrey's Pond, said, "I hear your brother's back," I wasn't exactly thrilled.

"Is he going to the high school next year?" she asked.

"I really don't know."

"I hope he does . . . he's so cute . . . and I love his sense of humor." Dana has been going with Jeremy Dragon since Christmas. They fight a lot and sometimes break up, but they always get back together. So why this sudden interest in my brother?

The bus came along then and I got on with Stephanie and Alison.

"Now I'm *really* curious," Alison said, as we took our usual seats. "I've got to meet this brother of yours!"

"How can you be so cruel and hateful?" I spoke

louder than I'd intended and some kids turned to look at me. So I lowered my voice to a whisper. "You're supposed to be my friend."

"I am your friend," Alison said. "And I think it's cruel and hateful of you to accuse me of being cruel and hateful, because I'm not!" She looked at Stephanie, who kind of shrugged at her.

"I just don't think I can take any more of this!" I felt very weak and leaned back against my seat, closing my eyes for a minute.

"Any more of what?" Alison asked.

"I think she's depressed about her brother," Stephanie told Alison, as if I couldn't hear.

"I know that," Alison said. "I'm not stupid." She fussed with her bag for a minute. She carries this huge canvas tote stuffed with all kinds of junk. She pulled out a roll of Lifesavers and offered one to Steph, then to me. I shook my head. Steph popped one into her mouth.

At the next stop Jeremy Dragon got on the bus. "Hey, Macbeth . . ." he said as he passed us. Last Halloween the three of us went to his house dressed as the witches from Shakespeare's play. When Jeremy came to the door, instead of saying *trick or treat*, we'd recited a poem.

Double, double, toil and trouble;
Fire burn and cauldron bubble.

And ever since, he's called us Macbeth. Sometimes it means all three of us—sometimes, like in math class, it's just me.

When we were moving again, Alison said, "I wonder what *my* brother's going to be like?"

"Your brother's going to be a baby," Stephanie reminded her.

For some reason that made me laugh. But my laugh came out high-pitched, not at all like my regular laugh.

"I wasn't trying to be funny," Steph told me. "I was just making a point."

"Are you saying that baby brothers aren't as depressing as older ones?" Alison asked.

"Not *all* older brothers are depressing," I said. "Just some."

Stephanie sighed. "Maybe you should see Mrs. Balaban."

"The school counselor?" I asked.

"Yeah," Steph said. "I saw her once . . . when I found out . . ." She hesitated for a moment. "When I found out my parents were separating."

"You went to Mrs. Balaban?" Alison said, as if she couldn't believe it.

Stephanie nodded.

"So did I!" Alison told her.

"You?" Steph said to Alison, as if *she* couldn't believe it. "Why did *you* go to Mrs. Balaban?"

"Because of the . . . when I found out about the . . ."

"Pregnancy?" I guessed.

"Right. . . . When I found out my mother was pregnant."

"How come you didn't *say* anything about seeing Mrs. Balaban?" Steph asked Alison.

"How come *you* didn't?" Alison asked Steph.

"I thought we were talking about *my* problem," I said, and they both looked at me.

The next morning Mrs. Balaban sent a note to my homeroom teacher, saying she wanted to see me. I was really angry. How could Alison and Stephanie betray me this way? If I want to see Mrs. Balaban, I will. But that's *my* business and nobody else's. I intended to tell them exactly that at lunch, which is our first and only period together except for gym, which we have twice a week but not today.

I stopped at Mrs. Balaban's office on my way to the cafeteria. "I'm Rachel Robinson," I said. "You wanted to see me?"

"Oh, Rachel . . . yes . . . I'm very glad to meet you," she said. "Sit down."

Mrs. Balaban is young and good-looking. The boys think it's great to be called to her office. One time she brought her baby, Hilary, to school. The girls oohed and aahed over her, while the boys oohed and aahed over Mrs. Balaban.

"I only have a minute," I said, standing in front of her desk. "I have to go to lunch."

"Well, let's see how fast I can explain this to you." She poured some sparkling water into a mug decorated with Beatrix Potter rabbits. "Want some?"

"No thanks."

She took a long drink. When she finished, she burped softly, her hand covering her mouth. "Sorry," she said. "Have you heard anything about Natural Helpers, Rachel?"

"I've heard of Natural Lime Spritzers," I answered.

She laughed. "This isn't a drink. It's a program we're going to try next fall. It's called Natural Helpers."

I felt my face turn hot. That's the kind of mistake Stephanie would make, not me. And it happened because I was worrying instead of listening.

"It's a kind of outreach program," Mrs. Balaban continued. "You know . . . kids helping other kids."

I waited to hear what this program had to do with Charles.

Mrs. Balaban took another swig from her cup. "I asked the teachers to recommend a group of mature seventh and eighth graders . . . people other kids would relate to . . . and you were one of them."

"So this doesn't have anything to do with . . ." I began.

"With . . ." Mrs. Balaban repeated, looking at me.

"Never mind. I was confused for a minute. I thought you wanted to see me because . . ."

"Because . . ."

I was so relieved this didn't have anything to do with Charles, I started to laugh.

"What?" she asked, curious.

"Nothing," I said, trying to keep a straight face.

She twirled her wedding band around on her finger. "Do you think you'd be interested in participating in this kind of program, Rachel?"

When I didn't respond right away, she said, "Of course I want you to take your time and think about it. Because the training will be fairly intense. And I know you're already involved in other school activities, not to mention your schoolwork."

"Schoolwork is no problem," I said.

She shuffled some papers on her desk. "Straight A's," she said, smiling up at me. She must have had my transcript in front of her. "Very impressive. But you know, Rachel, there's nothing wrong with a B now and then."

"I prefer A's," I said.

She laughed. "Remember, I don't want you to feel pressured to take this on, unless it's something you really want to do . . . okay?"

"Okay."

"We're having an introductory meeting next week, and Rachel . . ."

"Yes?"

"There's no rule that says Natural Helpers can't have their own problems . . . so if there's something on your mind that you'd like to talk about . . ."

"No," I said, "there's nothing."

"But if there ever is . . ."

"I have to go now," I told her. "This is my lunch period."

When I got to the cafeteria, Stephanie and Alison were already eating.

"Where were you?" Steph asked.

"Mrs. Balaban," I said.

"You actually took my advice?" she asked.

"Not exactly . . ."

Steph turned to Alison. "I knew she'd never admit she took *my* advice!"

My life at home is falling apart and Mrs. Balaban wants me to help other kids. What an incredible joke! What makes her think kids would come to me with their problems? I'm not very popular, except right before a test when everyone suddenly needs extra help. And when Steph's parents were separating, she didn't even *tell* me and I'm supposed to be her best friend! We had a huge fight when I found out she'd been lying to me. We didn't speak for seven weeks. And did Alison come to me when she found out her mother was pregnant? No. She went directly to Stephanie. So, it seems to me Mrs. Balaban doesn't know much about finding Natural Helpers!

That night I had too many *what ifs*. I knew I'd never get to sleep if I couldn't clear my head. So I went down to the kitchen to make myself a cup of herbal tea.

Charles was at the table, stuffing his face with cold mashed potatoes and leftover salmon with a big glob of mayonnaise on top. He'd refused to have dinner with us earlier. The thought of all that mayonnaise at ten o'clock at night was enough to gag me. I looked away and thought about going back upstairs. But then I changed my mind. Just because *he's* in the kitchen doesn't mean I can't have my tea. I took a few deep breaths and put the kettle on. While I was waiting for the water to boil, I opened the cupboard where we keep the teas and chose Grandma's Tummy Mint. Burt and Harry were sniffing around the table, begging for salmon.

"Come on, you guys," Charles said to them, with a mouthful of mashed potatoes. "Not while I'm eating."

"Cold mashed potatoes are disgusting," I muttered.

"To each his own," he said.

I didn't respond.

"You know . . . I'm worried about you, Rachel."

"You're worried about me?"

"Yeah . . . it's not normal for a girl your age not to have friends."

"I have plenty of friends."

"So where are they? How come they never come over?"

I chose my favorite mug, decorated with pink and lavender hearts, and poured boiling water over my tea bag. Then I set the mug down so the tea could steep. It's amazing how few people know how to make a good cup of tea. They think they can hand you a cup of hot water with a tea bag on the side and that's it.

"I asked you a question, Rachel."

"My friends are none of your business," I told him.

"I think you're trying to hide something."

I spun around. "I am *not* trying to hide anything. And I don't have to explain my friendships to you!" I knew better than to continue this conversation. So I took my tea upstairs, to the privacy of my own room.

The next day I asked Stephanie and Alison if they wanted to come over after school.

"Sure . . ." Alison said. "Will Charles be there?"

"Probably," I told her. "But don't get into a long conversation with him. Don't start telling him about your dog and how she can talk."

"Would he believe me if I did?" Alison asked.

"No, but he'd lead you on and then he'd never let you forget you said it."

"Fine . . . I won't say anything," Alison said.

"No . . . that would be even worse. Then he'll think you *can't* talk."

"Okay . . . I'll just say one or two things."

"And nothing personal," I told her. "Don't tell him your mother's pregnant."

"Got it," Alison said. "Nothing personal."

"And no questions!"

Alison repeated that. "No questions."

"You, too," I told Steph.

"All right," Steph said. "Stop worrying! I've known Charles since I was seven . . . remember?"

"I'm not worrying," I said.

The cats were sleeping outside the kitchen door when we got home. Burt woke up and stretched when he heard us. Harry didn't even move. I gave them fresh water from the outside faucet. Then I opened the door. Charles wasn't in the kitchen, so I poured three glasses of cranberry juice and set out a box of Dutch pretzels.

"The way you eat pretzels is so weird," Stephanie said to me.

"To each her own," I answered. It's true that I have a special way of eating pretzels. I like to lick off all the salt first. Then, when the pretzel is very soft, just before it's actually soggy, I chew it up. I didn't always eat pretzels that way. But a few years ago I broke a tooth on one, and ever since I eat them very carefully.

"Well . . . are we going to see him or not?" Alison finally asked.

"All right," I said. And I started down the hall to Charles's room, with Alison and Stephanie right behind me. I knocked and called, "Charles, I'm home with my friends!"

We waited but he didn't answer.

"Maybe he's not here," Steph said.

"I couldn't be so lucky," I mumbled on the way back to the kitchen. Just when I decided he probably wasn't home he appeared, fresh out of the shower, barefoot, with wet hair. He was wearing cutoffs and a T-shirt that said ELVIS IS DEAD.

"Well, well, well . . ." He smiled, surveying the scene.

I said, "Alison, this is my brother, Charles."

"You're Charles?" Alison said, like she couldn't believe it. What was she expecting . . . Dracula?

"None other," he answered, turning on the charm. "And who are you?"

"Alison Monceau." She practically drooled. "From L.A. I've heard a lot about you."

"I can imagine," Charles said. "I'm one of my sister's favorite subjects."

"Not from Rachel," Alison said quickly. "Rachel doesn't like to talk about you."

"What?" Charles said. "Impossible! Rachel, is this true? You don't talk about me anymore? You don't tell people how I bit you on your leg when you were two?"

"He bit you?" Alison asked me. Before I could answer, Stephanie waved her arms, trying to capture Charles's attention. "Hey," she called, "remember me?"

He looked her up and down. "No!" he said. "I don't believe it! This can't be Stephanie Hirsch!"

Stephanie suddenly grew self-conscious, touching her hair, her mouth, then crossing her arms over her chest. She tried to smile at him without showing her braces.

He was doing such a number on them! And they were just eating it up. Fools! I wanted to shout. He's just using you. He's just playing games.

"I was beginning to think the child prodigy had no friends," Charles said, making me cringe. "Why, just last night I accused her of being friendless. Right, Rachel?"

"That's it!" I said. "The party's over!"

I opened the screen door and let it slam behind me, expecting my friends to follow. But they just stood there, enthralled by my brother, until he said, " 'Parting is such sweet sorrow . . .' " and disappeared down the hall. As soon as he was gone, Stephanie and Alison burst out laughing.

"I don't see anything funny!" I told them from the other side of the screen door.

"That's your problem, Rachel," Stephanie said. She pushed the screen door open and she and Alison joined me outside. "Maybe if you treated him better, he'd treat you better."

"Why are you taking *his* side?" I asked. "You're supposed to be *my* friend."

"I am your friend," Steph argued.

"No," I said, "a friend is someone you can depend on!"

"You *can* depend on me. It's just that you always think everything's going to be a disaster!"

"Not everything," I told her. "Just *some* things!" But it was useless. They'd never understand. I turned and ran to the top of the hill. Then I lay on the grass with my arms hugging my body, and I began to roll. I rolled all the way down, like I used to when I was small, stopping myself just short of the pond.

Alison and Steph, thinking I was playing some game, followed, rolling down the hill after me, laughing hysterically. Steph stopped on her own, but I had to grab Alison or she'd have rolled right into the water. When she stood up, I steadied her. "Well . . ." I said, "are you satisfied?"

"About what?" she asked. Sometimes Alison is so dense!

"About Charles," I said.

"Oh, yeah . . . I guess." She and Steph exchanged looks. "I mean, based on what I just saw, I can see how he'd be a pain as a brother . . . but as a boy . . ."

I held up my hand. "I don't want to hear it, Alison!"

"All she's saying is—" Steph began.

But I didn't let her finish. "I am not interested in either of your opinions about my brother."

"It's getting hard to be around you, Rachel!" Steph said. "You're so . . . intense!" She turned to Alison. "Come on . . . let's go." And they walked off together.

I wanted to call after them, to tell them I needed them. But I couldn't find the words.

Instead I went home and rearranged my dresser drawers, folding and refolding each sweater, each T-shirt, each pair of socks. Then I started on my closet. When everything was in order, when everything was perfect, I sat down at my music stand, picked up my flute and began to play.

EIGHT

handed in my biography. I thought of taking out
the section about inventing a vaccine to prevent
hair balls in lions, but I didn't. Just because Charles
found it wildly funny or even peculiar doesn't mean
anything. Because Charles is peculiar himself.

He stays up all night watching reruns of old sitcoms
on TV—"The Munsters," "Gilligan's Island," "The
Brady Bunch." He goes to bed at sunrise and sleeps
away half the day. It's easy to avoid him on this
schedule. Maybe that's why he does it. Maybe he's
trying to avoid us. He doesn't even join us for dinner,
which is fine with Jessica and me. But it bothers
Mom and Dad. They think eating dinner together is
the single most important part of family life. They've
been seeing Dr. Sparks. They want Charles to see him
again, too, but so far he's refused.

"That quack!" Charles shouted at Mom a couple of

nights ago. "He knows *nothing*! You're blowing your money on him."

"Fine," Mom said, without raising her voice. "Then we'll find someone else. Someone you feel more comfortable with."

"Don't count on it," Charles told her.

At the dinner table we don't talk about him. Jess and I try to keep the conversation light, but you can tell Mom is stressed-out and Dad's not himself, either. He tries not to let us see he's distracted, but he can't fool me. I've seen him gobbling Pepto-Bismol tablets. And I've heard him talking quietly with Mom late at night, long after they're usually asleep. I've stopped asking them about Charles and what's going to happen, but I haven't stopped wondering if we have to live this way until he's eighteen.

On Monday my biography came back marked A+, and in the margin Ms. Lefferts wrote, *Excellent work, well thought out, delightful reading. See me.* When I went up to her after class, she said, "Rachel, I had no idea you were interested in the theater."

She was referring to my imagined career as a great actress. I'd written that Rachel died onstage at the age of ninety-seven. It was weird writing about my own death, but I suppose if I absolutely have to die—and death is a fact of life, isn't it?—then ninety-seven isn't bad, especially if I'm able to work right up to the end. Besides, since I'm just thirteen now, that gives me another eighty-four years to figure things out.

Ms. Lefferts was in one of her hyper moods, talking very fast, using her hands to punctuate every word. "I'm going to be advisor to the Drama Club next year and I certainly hope you'll join."

"Well . . ." I began.

But she didn't wait for me to finish. "I know you're busy. I recommended you for that helping program myself. . . . What's it called again?"

"Natural Helpers," I said.

"Yes, Natural Helpers . . . but the Drama Club could be a very exciting experience for you. We're going to do a fall play and a spring musical."

"I'll—"

"That's all I'm asking. That you give it your serious consideration. Because we really need people like you . . . people with a *genuine* interest in theater."

"It sounds—"

"Oh . . . and I forgot to mention we'll be going to New York to see at least two plays."

"Will we go by train or bus?" I asked.

She seemed surprised by my question. "I haven't worked that out yet. Do you have a preference?"

"Yes," I told her. "I prefer the train." I didn't add that I get motion sick in cars and buses but not on trains.

"Well . . ." she said, "I'll keep your preference in

mind. I'm hoping to get tickets to a contemporary drama and a Shakespearean comedy."

"Shakespeare is my favorite," I said.

Ms. Lefferts put her hand on my shoulder and squeezed lightly. "Mine, too, Rachel. Mine, too."

What am I going to do about all these activities? I wondered as I got into bed that night. Mom says the trick is to know your own limits. But I don't know what my limits are. I wish my teachers wouldn't expect me to do everything!

I decided to make a list. In one column I wrote down the activities I'm participating in now—Orchestral Band, All-State Orchestra, Debating Team, plus a private flute lesson each week and forty-five minutes of practice a day. In the other column I wrote down the activities I'm thinking about adding next year—Drama Club and Natural Helpers. Also, Stephanie wants me to run for eighth-grade class president. She's already volunteered to be my campaign manager and she's thought up the perfect slogan—*Rachel Robinson, the Dare to Care Candidate.*

I tried to figure out how many hours a week these activities would take, not counting president, but until tomorrow, when I go to the introductory meeting of Natural Helpers, I won't really be able to come up with an exact figure. I wonder if it's even possible to handle so many activities. I wish I could be a regular person for just one year! But then Mom would be disappointed. She'd say it's a crime to waste my potential. I wonder if she's ever wished she could be a regular person.

I turned off the light and lay down. Burt snuggled up against my hip and Harry at my feet. I closed my eyes, but my mind was on overtime. What if class president isn't allowed to participate in other activities? What if Natural Helpers turns out to be a full-time activity? What if I get a part in the school play, which means rehearsals every afternoon, when I'm supposed to be at Debating Club preparing for an interschool match and Orchestral Band is rehearsing for the spring concert and my flute teacher says I haven't been practicing enough and my grades start slipping and everybody says I'm not doing my job as class president because I'm too busy doing other things and I am impeached by the class officers? Being impeached would be even worse than being expelled. Being impeached would probably make the local papers!

Suddenly I felt my heart thumping inside my chest. I sat straight up, frightened. The cats looked at me as I leaped out of bed. But then a voice inside my head reminded me to stay calm, to breathe deeply. I began to count backward from one hundred. That's it . . . count slowly . . . very slowly . . . that's better . . .

The panicky feeling passed, leaving me drenched

with sweat. I lay back down and closed my eyes. *Psychology Today* says one good relaxation technique is to imagine yourself in a serene setting, like a beautiful tropical island with a white sand beach and palm trees swaying gently in the warm breeze. Yes. Okay. I'm on an island, swinging in a hammock, when this incredibly handsome guy comes up to me. He's carrying a book of Shakespeare's sonnets. He sits beside me and begins to read. After a while he reaches for my hand, looks deep into my eyes and, not being able to resist a moment longer, kisses me. It is a long, passionate kiss . . . without tongues. The idea of having someone's tongue in my mouth is too disgusting to contemplate.

I must have fallen asleep then, but when I awoke in the morning I had a gnawing ache in my jaw.

The next afternoon I went to the introductory meeting of Natural Helpers and nearly passed out when Mrs. Balaban presented someone named Dr. Sparks. Could he be *that* Dr. Sparks? I wondered, as I slid lower and lower in my seat. How many psychologists named Dr. Sparks can there be in one town? He must be the same one! Suppose he recognizes my name and asks if I'm related to Charles? Suppose he tells Mrs. Balaban that with my family situation I shouldn't be a Natural Helper?

I worried all through the meeting. I hardly heard a word he said.

But when the meeting ended, Mrs. Balaban thanked Dr. Sparks and he left without addressing any of us individually. I felt so relieved I let out a low sigh. Only the girl next to me seemed to notice. Then Mrs. Balaban told us we should think long and hard about becoming Natural Helpers. "I'll need your answer by the last day of school," she said. "And remember, it's a significant commitment. Helping others always is. You'll have to be aware and involved all the time."

Aware and involved all the time, I thought as I sat in the dentist's office after school. By then my jaw was killing me. I opened and closed my mouth, hoping to relieve the pain.

Unlike most of my friends, I'm not afraid to go to the dentist. I have very healthy teeth. I've had just two small cavities in my entire life. Besides, our dentist, Dr. McKay, is also a stand-up comic. He performs at the Laugh Track, a comedy club on the highway. He tries out his material on his patients, so in this case you might say, going to the dentist is a lot of laughs!

"So, Rachel . . . how do you get down from an elephant?" Dr. McKay asked as he adjusted the towel around my neck.

"I've no idea," I told him.

He tilted the chair way back. "You don't . . . you get it from a duck."

I laughed, which wasn't easy to do with my mouth

open and the dentist's hands inside. I hate the taste of his white surgical gloves.

"Hmm . . ." he said, poking around. "Are you wearing your appliance?"

I tried to explain that I'd lost it, but he couldn't understand me. I guess he got the general tone, though, because he said, "So, the answer is no?"

I nodded.

"Well, you're clenching your jaw again."

I tried to act surprised. I said, "I am?" It came out sounding like *Ah aah?*

"Uh-huh . . ." he said. "And grinding your teeth, too."

Grinding my teeth? That definitely did not sound good.

"Everything all right in your life?" he asked.

I wiggled my fingers, indicating so-so.

"Still getting all A's in school?"

I wish people would stop acting as if there's something wrong with getting all A's. I waved my hands around, our signal for letting me sit up and rinse. After I did, I said, "This doesn't have anything to do with school."

"Maybe not, but I'd still like to see you learn to relax. And so would your teeth."

People are always telling me to relax, as if it's something easy to do. When Dr. McKay finished cleaning my teeth, he moved the chair to an upright position. "I'm going to do an impression," he said.

I assumed he meant an impression of someone famous. So I was surprised when he said, "Open wide, Rachel . . ." and he slid a little tray of flavored goo into my mouth.

On the way out of Dr. McKay's office I met Steph, who had an appointment with the orthodontist in the next office. "How do you get down from an elephant?" I asked. I hardly ever tell jokes because no one laughs when I do. I don't know if this means my comic timing is off or people just don't expect me to be funny.

"How?" Steph said.

"You don't. You get it from a duck."

Steph just looked at me.

"It's a joke," I said. "Down . . . as in feathers. Get it?"

"Oh, right . . ." Steph said. "Now I do." But she didn't laugh. Then she said, "Did you hear about Marcella, the eighth-grade slut?"

"No, what?"

"She got caught in the supply closet with Jeremy Dragon."

"Is this a joke?"

"No. Why would it be a joke?"

"I don't know. The way you set it up, I thought you were going to tell a joke."

"No, this is a true story," Steph said. "It was the

supply closet in the arts center. When Dana found out she went crazy, yelling and screaming in front of everyone!"

"Really?"

"Yes . . . then Jeremy goes, 'How come it's okay for you but not for me?' And Dana shouts, 'What are you talking about?' Then Jeremy goes, 'You know what I'm talking about!' And he walks away, which makes Dana so mad she takes off his bracelet and throws it at him. It hits him in the back of his head. So he turns around and goes, 'Thanks, Dana!' Then he picks up his bracelet and puts it in his pocket."

"You were actually there?" I asked. "You actually saw this happen?"

"No," Steph said. "But everybody's talking about it. Everybody knows!"

"What was he doing in the supply closet with Marcella?"

"What do you think?" Before I had a chance to respond, Steph answered her own question. "Pure animal attraction!"

"Yes, but the difference between humans and animals is that humans are supposed to *think*," I explained, "not just react."

"But let's say you were alone in a supply closet with Jeremy Dragon . . ." Steph said. "Wouldn't you react?"

"I don't know."

"Well, I do. I'm reacting just thinking about it, like any normal person."

"Are you suggesting I'm not normal?"

"I didn't say that."

"It sounded like you did."

"Well, I didn't."

"Good, because I'm as normal as you!"

"If you say so."

"What do you mean by that?"

"Lighten up, Rachel, will you?" Stephanie said, shaking her head. "You're never going to make it to eighth grade at this rate."

I wanted to ask Steph exactly what she meant by that remark, but she went into the orthodontist's office before I had the chance. It's not as if I wouldn't want to be alone with Jeremy Dragon. But I'd choose someplace more romantic than a supply closet at school!

NINE

When Alison came over that night, I asked if she'd heard about Jeremy Dragon and Marcella. "Steph told me," she said. "I feel bad for Dana." She walked around my room touching things—the framed photos on my dresser, my collection of decorated boxes, the needlepoint pillows on my bed. "I'd do anything for a room like this." She sounded as if she were in a trance.

Since she goes through this routine every time, I decided to call her on it. "Okay," I said, "on Saturday I'm coming over and we're going to organize your room."

"Oh no," Alison said, "it wouldn't work!"

"Why not?"

"I'd never be able to keep it like . . . this," she said, opening my closet door, "with all my clothes facing the same direction, and my shoes lined up in a row."

"It's easy!" I told her. "You just have to put away your clothes when you take them off."

"But you know how I am. You know I never put anything away until my closet is empty and all my clothes are piled on the floor."

"You can do it if you want to."

"I want to . . . but I know myself. I'm too tired at night to care."

"Then you should go to bed earlier."

"That's what my mother says."

"I don't mean to sound like your mother, but you'll never know until you try."

"No, I'd just wind up feeling bad." She sighed. "Maybe someday. Maybe next year, okay?"

I shrugged. "Whenever."

"Besides," she said, looking around, "Steph says it isn't normal for a teenager to have a room as perfect as this."

"Stephanie said that . . . about me?"

"Not about you," Alison said, backing off. "About your room. We were just talking, you know, about this article in *Sassy* and . . ." I waited while she painted herself into a corner. "Steph didn't mean it personally or anything."

"I cannot believe Stephanie told you I'm not normal."

"She didn't say that!"

"You know what Stephanie's problem is?" I asked.

"Stephanie confuses *normal* with *average*. It's true that the *average* teenager doesn't keep her room as neat as I keep mine. But just because it isn't *average* doesn't mean it's not *normal*."

I absolutely detest the word *normal*. I detest the way Stephanie throws it around. And, I admit, sometimes I do wonder about myself. There's no question, I'm different from most kids my age. I don't know how to explain it. Maybe when my mother jokes to her friends that *Rachel was born thirty-five*, she knows what she's talking about. Maybe I won't find out until I actually *am* thirty-five. Maybe then I'll be more like everyone else.

Alison was running her hand over the books on my shelves. "So, can you recommend something good? I have a book report due on Friday and I forgot to go to the library."

"They're all good," I told her. "It just depends on what you're in the mood for."

"Something about a girl who lived a long time ago."

"Historical fiction," I translated. "Let me think . . ." My books are arranged alphabetically by author so I know exactly where each one is. I pulled two off my shelf—*Summer of My German Soldier* and *A Tree Grows in Brooklyn*—and handed them to Alison.

"I'll take this one," she said, thumbing through the first.

"Good choice," I told her. "I think you'll like it." I wrote down Alison's name, followed by the title and author, in my library notebook. Even though every one of my books has a bookplate on the inside cover, some people forget to return them. They don't mean to. It just happens. This way I know who's got what. As I was putting away my notebook, Charles opened my bedroom door. "You know you're supposed to knock!" I said.

But he paid no attention. "I was hoping for a quick game of *torture*," he said, standing in the doorway.

"We are *not* interested!" I tried to force him out by closing the door but he blocked it.

"What's *torture*?" Alison asked.

"*Torture* is having a conversation with my brother. *Torture* is enduring his witty comments."

Alison didn't get it. But Charles pushed past me and said, "An excellent definition, Rachel." He looked at Alison. "You just don't know how refreshing it is to live with a child prodigy."

Alison didn't get that, either. She sat on the edge of my bed, not knowing what to say. Charles smiled at her. She smiled back, clearly flattered by his attention.

"So, what's your ethnic heritage, California?" he asked.

"None of your business," I told him, answering for Alison.

"I don't mean to pry," Charles said to her smoothly, "but I'm very interested in ethnic heritage, given my background."

What background? I wondered.

"Well, I'm adopted," Alison said. "I don't know anything except that my birth mother was Vietnamese."

"I'm adopted, too," Charles said. "I wish our family were as open about it as yours."

"What are you saying?" I asked, totally shocked. "You're not adopted!"

"You mean you never guessed?" he asked me. "You never put two and two together?"

"You're lying!" I shouted. Then I turned to Alison. "He's lying!"

"Here are the facts," Charles said quietly to Alison, as he sat beside her on my bed. "I'm one-eighth Korean, one-eighth Native American, one-quarter Irish, one-quarter Eastern European, and one-quarter Cuban."

"How would you know all that if you were adopted?" I asked.

"I've seen the papers."

Alison was confused and so was I. "Get out of my room!" I shouted at Charles, holding the door open. "Now!"

"Good-night, California," Charles sang as he left. "Until next time . . ." He blew her a kiss.

I slammed the door after him. "I'm sorry," I said to Alison. "He's so obnoxious."

"No . . . it's okay," she said.

"It's not okay! He's playing with your mind."

"Maybe he is adopted."

"He's not!"

"You're younger," she said. "Maybe you just don't know. Some people don't talk about it."

"It's not possible!" I said, feeling lost. "Grandpa Robinson said—" I stopped in midsentence. "I mean, he looks like my father . . . don't you think?"

"Not really," she said.

But Mom and Dad would never keep such a secret, would they? No, they believe in honesty. On the other hand, Mom is a very private person. She holds everything inside.

As soon as Alison left, I went directly to my parents' room and knocked on their door.

Dad called, "Enter. . . ." He was grading papers at his desk. I heard water running in the bathroom. Mom was probably taking a shower.

I pulled a small chair over to Dad's desk and waited for him to look up from his work. When he did, he said, "What can I do for you?"

"I have a very important question," I said.

"Okay . . . shoot."

There was no easy way to do this. I focused on Mom's collection of glass bottles. There are eleven of them sitting on top of her dresser, each with a silver top.

"Rachel . . ." Dad said.

I looked at him, then back at Mom's bottles. Finally I managed to say, "Is Charles adopted?"

Dad didn't answer right away. He reached for my hand. "I know it must feel that way to you . . ."

"It doesn't feel that way to me," I said, "but that's what he just told Alison! He told her he's one-eighth Native American, one-eighth Korean, one-quarter Irish and . . ."

Dad started laughing.

"I don't find it funny at all!"

"He's not adopted," Dad said. "He probably just feels that would explain things."

"Are you absolutely sure?" I asked.

Dad stroked my arm. "I was there at his birth, honey. I held him in my arms, same as I held Jessica and you when you were born. Not that I wouldn't love any of you just as much if you were adopted . . ."

"It's cruel to lie to someone who really is adopted, trying to make her think they have something in common."

"I'm not excusing him," Dad said, "but maybe he likes Alison and is trying to impress her."

"What do you mean by *likes*?"

Dad kind of smiled and said, "You know . . . boy meets girl . . ."

"You mean likes her *that* way!" I didn't give Dad a chance to respond. I jumped up. "That's out of the question. She's my friend. My friends are off-limits to him. You've got to do something, Dad! You've got to get him out of my life!"

"Rachel, honey . . ." Dad stood, too, and wrapped me in his arms. "It's going to be all right. I know these are difficult times . . ."

"So were the Crusades!" Mom said, coming out of the bathroom in her purple robe.

TEN

Charles has a tutor. His name is Paul Medeiros and he's tall, about six feet, with dark hair and dark eyes. He wears rimless glasses. He's Dad's student teacher. He's going to come to our house every afternoon for two hours. This means Charles will *not* be finishing ninth grade at my school. What a relief!

When I met Paul a few days ago, he was wearing jeans and a black pocket T-shirt. He had a pencil smudge on the side of his face. He said, "So you're Charles's older sister."

"No," Charles told him, "this is my *baby* sister." Charles was wearing a T-shirt that said ALL STRESSED UP AND NO ONE TO CHOKE. I felt like choking him!

"She doesn't look like a baby," Paul said.

"Looks can be deceiving," Charles said. "She's just thirteen." He said *thirteen* as if it were the plague.

I could see the surprise on Paul's face. But I liked

him for not making a big thing out of it. "Then you're the musician?" Paul asked.

"Well, I love music but I'm not that good," I told him.

"She's only a child prodigy," Charles said.

"Charles . . . I am not!" I wish he would stop calling me that! I've met real prodigies at music camp. Some of them are only ten or eleven and they're already studying at Juilliard. It was a shock when I realized I'll never be as good as they are, no matter how much I practice.

Paul gave me an understanding smile, then playfully shoved Charles back toward his room. "Okay, time to hit the books." He turned for a moment and said, "Nice to meet you, Rachel."

When he said my name, I felt incredibly warm inside. At first I thought I was having what Mom and her friends call a *hot flash*. But I don't think you get them till you're older. I'm not sure if what I feel for Paul is pure animal attraction or not. Either way, from now on I'll have to be very careful because if Charles ever finds out—or even *suspects*—I have an interest in Paul, he will deliberately humiliate me in front of him. Not that I think Paul would let him get away with it. Still, the damage would be done.

That night I lay on my bed reading sonnets to the cats. I imagined I was onstage and the entire audience, including Paul, was mesmerized by my voice.

Suddenly I had the feeling I wasn't alone and when I looked up, Charles was standing in my doorway. "You read Shakespeare to the cats?" he asked.

"They're very good listeners," I told him. "Now please leave!"

"You know, Rachel . . . when people start reading to their animals . . ."

"Out!" I said again. "Right now!"

I could hear him chuckling even after he'd closed my door.

I began to think of Paul every night when I went to bed. Thinking about him is very relaxing. It's better than anything I've read in *Psychology Today*. My jaw hasn't hurt at all since Paul started coming to our house. But whether that's due to my new dental appliance or to Paul himself, I really can't say.

I wonder if Tarren knows him since he's graduating from the same college where she is a junior. Next time I see her I'll have to ask.

But the next time Tarren came over, she pressed a screaming baby into my arms and said, "Where's your mother?" Her eyes were red and swollen, her hair damp and matted around her face.

Mom was at the dining room table, working on what could be her last big jury trial before she is appointed a judge. "Tarren, what is it?" Mom asked, pushing back her chair.

Tarren threw her arms around Mom and cried, "Aunt Nell . . . my life is just one big mess! I don't think I can take it anymore."

Roddy continued to scream. Mom said, "Rachel, take the baby into the kitchen and give him a bottle or something."

Tarren pulled off her shoulder bag and passed it to me. "There's a bottle inside."

I took Roddy into the kitchen, but since there's no door between the kitchen and the dining room I could still hear everything.

"All right," Mom said to Tarren. "Now calm down and tell me what's going on."

Tarren sobbed, "I got another ticket . . . for speeding. I was only doing sixty-seven, but they gave me points." She blew her nose. "If I lose my license I won't be able to get to school and if I can't get to school I'll never graduate, and if I don't graduate and get a teaching job I'll never be able to support myself and Roddy and I'll never get out of my parents' house, or have my own life, or . . ." She was crying again.

Mom sounded firm. "Listen to me, Tarren. We've been through this before. You are responsible for your own actions."

"But it was a mistake," Tarren cried. "I didn't know I was going over the speed limit."

"We all make mistakes," Mom told her. "The point

is, you can't fall apart every time something goes wrong. You've got to learn to be strong!"

"I don't know how to be strong, Aunt Nell. I want to be like you . . . you know I do . . . but I just don't know how."

"Then you're going to learn, right now," Mom said. "You're going to start by telling yourself, This is not a life-threatening situation. This is not a serious problem."

"It's not?" Tarren asked.

"No, it's not!" Mom said.

Roddy lay in my arms, sucking on his bottle, his fingers playing with my hair. I love Roddy. I love the way he smells and feels. I love his sweetness.

"And I don't want to hear you sounding like your father, Tarren," Mom continued. "Your father still hasn't learned to be strong, and he's forty . . ." Mom hesitated.

"Forty-four," Tarren said.

"Yes, forty-four," Mom repeated. Mom says Uncle Carter takes after Grandfather Babcock, who drank too much and wasted his money on get-rich-quick schemes. I never knew Grandfather Babcock. He died when Mom was just nineteen. I think she worries that Charles will turn out like him or Uncle Carter.

"Life is an obstacle course," Mom said.

I know Mom's obstacle speech by heart. *We all have to make decisions. I'm not saying it's easy. But you don't have to collapse every time you come face-to-face with an obstacle.*

"An obstacle . . ." Tarren repeated, her voice trailing off.

As Mom and Tarren were talking, Charles breezed into the kitchen. "Hey, Roddy, baby . . . how's it going?" He lifted Roddy off my lap and held him high over his head. Roddy shrieked, loving it.

"He just finished a . . ." I began to say, but by then it was too late. Roddy spit up half of what I'd just fed him, right on Charles's head.

Charles shoved Roddy back at me and ran for the sink. He turned on the faucet full blast and stuck his head under it. When he'd had enough, he turned off the water and shook his head like a dog who's been for a swim. Roddy clapped his hands and laughed. Then Charles laughed, too. "Very funny, Roddy," he said. "Ha-ha-ha."

"Aa-aa-aa," Roddy sang back.

"So what's tonight's catastrophe?" Charles asked, with a nod in Tarren's direction. He grabbed a kitchen towel and wiped his face.

"A speeding ticket," I said.

"She thinks Mom can fix it?"

"I don't know."

"Lots of luck," Charles said. Then he waved at Roddy and left.

This is what it must be like to have a regular brother, I thought. Someone you can laugh with, someone who talks to you naturally, without being sarcastic or cruel. Someone you can face every day without feeling you are walking on eggs. Why can't Charles be that kind of brother all the time?

Tarren looked less anxious when she came back into the kitchen. "I don't know what I'd do without you, Aunt Nell." She hugged Mom. "You're the most supportive person in my life. I hope someday I'll be more like you."

"You'll be fine," Mom said. "You can handle whatever life throws your way. Remember . . . obstacles, not problems."

"Right," Tarren said. "Obstacles." She reached for Roddy.

"You are about the luckiest girl alive," she told me. "You have the most wonderful mother in the entire universe!"

It's funny how people think life would be perfect if only they had different parents.

ELEVEN

Jessica has hardly been home this week. She and her friends are looking for summer jobs. I saw them downtown this afternoon, while Steph, Alison and I were shopping for shorts and T-shirts. Jess and Kristen were inside Ed's car. They seemed to be having a heavy discussion, so I didn't wave or anything.

Later, when we sat down to dinner, Dad asked Jess how the job hunt was going. Jessica put down her fork. "I've been all over town. I've answered every help-wanted ad in the paper and I always get the same reaction. They take one look at my skin and say, 'Nothing available now.' One woman even whispered, 'Come back when your skin clears up, dear.' Can you believe it! I mean, is that discrimination or is that discrimination? I'm thinking of suing."

Jess caught the look that passed between Mom and Dad. "Well, why not?" she asked them. "You can sue for sex discrimination and race discrimination and other discriminations, so why *not* skin discrimination?"

Mom said, "It's a temporary condition, Jess. Painful, but temporary."

"Does that make it okay for people to treat me like a freak?" Jessica asked. "Maybe my skin will never clear up. Maybe no one will ever hire me for anything. Maybe I'll just wear a face mask for the rest of my life!"

"An interesting idea," Dad said, and we turned to him. "I mean," he said quickly, "the idea of discrimination based on a skin condition."

Jessica sat up, her eyes bright.

"Or could it be viewed as a disability?" Dad asked Mom.

Mom mulled that over while she chewed, then swallowed whatever was in her mouth. "The law says you can't discriminate against someone because of a disability," she said. "If we could prove that acne is a disability . . ."

"So you'll take my case?" Jessica asked Mom.

"As a judge I wouldn't be able to represent you, Jess."

We all stopped midmouthful and turned to Mom, who flushed.

"You heard?" Dad asked.

Mom nodded. "Today."

"Why didn't you say something?" I asked.

"I was waiting for the right moment," Mom said.

"Well," Dad said, "this calls for a special toast." He poured himself half a glass of wine and held it up. "To Nell Babcock Robinson, who will bring her sense of fair play and justice to the bench!"

Jess and I joined Dad in his toast, raising our water glasses to Mom. "Will you still have to finish your big case?" I asked.

"Yes, but this will be my last one as a trial lawyer." Then she said, "It'll mean a substantial cut in income."

"We'll manage," Dad said.

I love you, Mom mouthed at him.

I love you, too, Dad mouthed back.

"Does this mean we're not going to decide about my lawsuit?" Jess asked.

Mom snapped back to reality. "What I started to say, honey, is . . . as a judge I wouldn't be able to handle your case. Dad can talk to his friends at the Employment Rights Project. They might have some ideas for you."

"But not you!" Jess exploded. "Not my own mother, the greatest trial lawyer who ever lived. I'll bet you'd help Tarren, though, wouldn't you?"

Mom winced.

"Jessica . . ." Dad said, touching her hand.

"What?"

"That's not fair."

"Exactly!" Jess said.

Mom started to say, "Don't you think I know . . ."

But Jess got up from the table and marched into the kitchen with her plate.

Mom's face tightened but she continued to eat, taking very small bites.

Dad tried to reassure me. "She'll be all right," he said, knowing I was thinking about Jess. "She's just upset over not getting a job."

I nodded, trying not to show how close to tears I was, trying to eat the rest of my dinner exactly like Mom, cutting my food into tiny pieces so I barely had to chew.

On Friday night Stephanie invited Alison and me to her house for supper. Steph's mother came home from work with two pizzas—one plain and one with the works. She put them into the oven in their boxes, then went upstairs, calling, "Be down in a jiff."

Mrs. Hirsch is a lot younger than Mom. Her name is Rowena and she has permed hair and big eyes. She dresses in clothes that look like costumes. One day she'll wear a long peasant skirt—the next she's in western gear. She used to look more like your basic working woman, but since she and Mr. Hirsch split up she's become more exotic.

Steph's house is cluttered, with piles of magazines and papers waiting to be read, and odd pieces of furniture that don't make any sense, like the sink in the foyer. Mrs. Hirsch has taken off the cabinet doors in the kitchen, so everything, including cereal boxes, is right out in the open. Steph's father is the complete opposite of her mother. You wonder how they got married in the first place but not why they've split up.

Stephanie's brother, Bruce, is ten. He's a worrier, like me. He should have been *my* brother. "What's new?" I asked him, as we sat around the kitchen table.

"Only good news, Bruce!" Stephanie warned. "Nothing about the rain forest, endangered species, global warming or the homeless. We don't need any of your gloom and doom tonight."

Bruce thought that over and finally said, "The Mets beat the Cards ten–zip."

"You call that news!" Stephanie said.

"Yeah, I call that news," Bruce told her. "I call that very good news."

"I wonder if my brother's going to be a baseball fan," Alison said.

"Your brother's going to be a baby," Steph said.

"I wish you'd stop saying that!" Alison told her. "I was talking about when he's older."

Mrs. Hirsch came back into the kitchen wearing tight jeans and a lacy top. She pulled the pizza boxes out of the oven. They were beginning to smell like burned cardboard. She set them on the table and told us to help ourselves.

"Yum . . ." Alison said, taking the first bite.

As much as I enjoy pizza, I can't eat it without thinking about Jess and those obnoxious boys who call her Pizza Face.

As if Mrs. Hirsch could read my mind, she suddenly asked, "How's Jessica?"

"She's trying to get a job," I said, "but so far she hasn't had any luck."

"Tell her to give me a call," Mrs. Hirsch said. "I'm looking for someone intelligent and responsible." Mrs. Hirsch owns a travel agency in town. It's called Going Places.

"Jess is very intelligent and responsible," I told Mrs. Hirsch.

"I know that," she said. "I wouldn't expect anything less from your family, Rachel." She turned to Alison. "And how's it going with *your* mom? Is she feeling okay?"

"She says she feels fat," Alison said. "She can't see her toes in the shower."

Mrs. Hirsch laughed. "When is the baby due?"

"July eleventh."

"Tell your folks if there's anything I can do, just give me a call," Mrs. Hirsch said. "Now, who's ready for a second slice?"

We all answered at once.

When we'd polished off both pizzas, Stephanie carried a plate of brownies to the table. "Well . . ." her mother said, "as long as you're all here together, I may just run out for an hour or two."

"Where to?" Steph asked.

"To see a friend."

"What friend?"

"Really, Steph . . ." Mrs. Hirsch said, with half a laugh.

"Really, what?" Steph asked, shoving most of the brownie into her mouth at once.

"If you don't want me to go out, I won't," Mrs. Hirsch told her.

"Did I say that?" Steph looked around the table. "Did anyone hear me say that?"

None of us answered.

"I just want to know *what* friend you're going to see," Steph continued. "And I want a number where I can reach you. You *said* we should always have a number, just in case, remember?"

"Yes," her mother said, "I remember."

Alison and I exchanged glances as Mrs. Hirsch pulled the phone book out of a drawer and thumbed through it. She jotted down a number and handed it to Steph. Steph looked it over, then asked, "Who is Geoff Boseman?"

"A friend," Mrs. Hirsch said.

"I never heard of him."

Mrs. Hirsch sighed. "He's a new friend."

"You mean this is a date?"

"Not unless you call two friends having coffee together a date."

"I do if one is a man and one is a woman."

"You're overreacting, Steph," Mrs. Hirsch said. She
dropped a kiss on Bruce's cheek, but when she tried
to kiss Stephanie, Steph ducked and Mrs. Hirsch
wound up kissing air. She gave Alison and me a kind
of embarrassed smile. "I'll be back in two hours, at
the latest. Keep everything locked." She grabbed her
purse and headed for the kitchen door.

When she was gone, Stephanie said, "You think I
was overreacting?"

"Yes," I said.

Then Steph looked at Alison, who nodded and
said, "She's separated. She's allowed to have dates.
But even if she was still married, she could meet a
friend for coffee, or even dinner."

"A friend that Bruce and I have never heard of?"

"I've heard of him," Bruce said.

"You've heard of Geoff, with a *G*, Boseman?" Steph
asked him.

"Yeah. Isn't he the guy Mom met at the gym?"

"The gym!" Steph said. "She's having coffee with
some guy she met at the gym?"

"On the StairMaster," Bruce said.

"The StairMaster?"

"I think that's what she said."

"I can't believe this!" Stephanie said to the ceiling.

"Lighten up," Bruce told Steph. Exactly what Steph is always telling me.

"Yeah," Alison said, "stepfathers can be the best. Look at Leon."

"I don't *need* a stepfather!" Stephanie said.

"Isn't this conversation premature?" I asked. "I mean, one cup of coffee does not necessarily lead to marriage." As soon as I said it, I realized my mistake. Natural Helpers are supposed to listen carefully, not just to the spoken but to the unspoken. We're supposed to acknowledge feelings. But did I acknowledge Stephanie's feelings? No, I did not. And did I size up the seriousness of the situation and offer support and encouragement? *No.* If I'm going to be a Natural Helper, I'm going to have to learn to be a better friend.

At eight, Steph and I sat down to watch Gena's TV show. It's called "Franny on Her Own," and it's the only show on TV I watch regularly. Actually it's not as bad as most half hour comedies. It doesn't have a laugh track and it's not stupid. Gena plays an intelligent woman who comes to live in the city after years in the country. It's a kind of city-mouse, country-mouse story. They finished shooting for the season before she looked pregnant. Alison says Gena would rather stay home with the baby next year, but it's hard to give up that kind of salary.

"This is so embarrassing," Alison said as the show began. "I don't see why you want to watch it."

"Because your mother is the star!" Steph explained. "We know her."

"Why don't you tape it instead?" Alison said. "Then we could do something interesting."

"It's just half an hour," Steph told her. "You can read or something if you don't want to watch."

"Or play computer games with me!" Bruce said. "I couldn't care less about your mother's TV show."

"You're on!" Alison told him, and the two of them ran up to his room while Steph and I laughed over "Franny on Her Own." It felt good to laugh with Steph again. According to *Psychology Today*, laughter is the best medicine.

TWELVE

Jessica got the job at Going Places. She'll be working full-time over the summer but just three afternoons, plus Saturdays, for now. After her first day of work she was bubbling with excitement, not just about the job but about Mrs. Hirsch. "*Rowena* . . . isn't that the most romantic name?" she said on Monday night. She was on the living room floor surrounded by travel brochures. "She's so warm."

"Who is?" Charles asked. He was passing through with a copy of Stephen King's latest book. Stephen King is his hero. Maybe he can go live with him in Maine!

Jessica looked up at Charles. "I was talking about Rowena Hirsch, my boss."

Mom came through then, with a mug of coffee. "What about her?" she asked.

"I was just saying how *warm* she is," Jess repeated.

"How sincere. She's completely different from anyone I've ever known."

Mom raised her eyebrows but didn't comment.

"I'm thinking of becoming a travel agent," Jess said. "I mean, not right now, but later, when I finish college. I'd love to travel."

"Travel agents don't get to travel," I told Jess. "They arrange for other people to travel."

"Rowena doesn't travel much because she has kids at home," Jess said. "But there's another agent at her office who travels all the time. She writes a newsletter, reporting on hotels and stuff like that."

"You've only been working one day," Mom reminded her.

"You can tell a lot in one day," Jess said.

"A travel agent," Charles said. "That suits you, Jess."

"What do you mean by that?" Jessica asked, suddenly wary.

"I mean I can see you as a travel agent. You'd be very . . . competent."

Jessica didn't answer him. It's always hard to know when he's coming in for the kill.

"I'm glad you enjoyed your first day on the job," Mom said, "but shouldn't you be working on your English paper now?"

"It's not due until Friday."

"That doesn't give you much time."

Jess gathered up her travel brochures.

"And you've got the SAT's on Saturday morning," Mom reminded her. "I hope you've explained that to Rowena."

"I have . . . but they're just for practice."

"Still, you want to do your best, don't you?"

Jess muttered something under her breath and headed upstairs.

Charles tsk tsked. "It's not easy running your children's lives, is it, Mom?"

Mom gave him a look but didn't answer his question.

After Jessica's second day of work it was, "I love the way Rowena dresses. She has such style." The two of us were in the bathroom, brushing our teeth before bed. "And she built the business on her own. She's a real role model for today's young women."

"She's not that great," I said, annoyed at the way Jessica was gushing.

"I guess you really don't know Rowena the person, Rachel. You only know her as Stephanie's mother."

"You can tell a lot by how someone treats her children," I said. Not that I've ever seen Mrs. Hirsch treat Steph or Bruce badly, but she's not as perfect as Jessica thinks, either.

By the end of Jessica's first week of work we were all sick of hearing about Rowena and we'd pretty much tuned her out until she said, "And Rowena thinks I should be taking Accutane now." Mom and

Dad were at the kitchen table finishing their coffee and going over the household bills. Jess and I were drying the pots and pans from dinner. "She doesn't see any point in waiting and neither do I. She even gave me an article about it. Here . . ." Jess said, pulling a folded page from a magazine out of her pocket and shoving it under Mom's nose. "Her nephew's acne cleared up six weeks after he started taking it. *Six weeks!* And he hasn't had any side effects at all." She looked from Dad to Mom, then continued, "And with my salary I can pay for it on my own. Rowena even said she'd give me an advance, if I need it."

"Where did you get the idea we can't afford Accutane?" Mom asked.

"Well, it's expensive," Jess said. "And you've been making such a big thing out of your *substantial* cut in income now that you're going to be a judge."

"It's the serious side effects that concern me," Mom said, "not the cost. Our insurance would cover the cost."

Jess exploded. "The truth is, you don't want me to take it. You've never wanted me to take it!"

"Jessica, that's just not true," Mom said. "Accutane isn't a drug to take casually. Maybe Rowena doesn't know that. I'm going to call and straighten this out right now!"

"Nell . . ." Dad said.

"Don't *Nell* me," Mom told him, storming out of

the kitchen. Dad followed her into the living room.

"Welcome to another evening of fun and games with the Robinsons," Charles said, appearing out of nowhere. He opened the freezer and pulled out an ice-cream sandwich.

"Just shut up!" Jessica shouted.

Charles smiled and went out the kitchen screen door, letting it slam behind him.

"I wish I lived at Rowena's!" Jess said to me.

"You sound like Tarren," I told her. "And you know how much you love it when she gets going over Mom."

"This has nothing to do with Tarren!" Jess said.

"Why are you angry at me?" I asked. "What'd I do?"

"I'm *not* angry at you. I'm angry at *them*," she said, with a nod in the direction of the living room, "for not taking me to someone else when Dr. Lucas said I should wait before I take Accutane. And now I find out I've been suffering for more than a year just because Mom has some warped idea that bad skin makes you a stronger person."

"Mom never said that."

"She doesn't have to say it, Rachel. You've heard it often enough, haven't you? *Looking back,*" Jess said, in a perfect imitation of Mom, "*I realize I am where I am today because I had very little social life during my teens due to bad skin. Bad skin has . . .*"

She stopped when she saw Mom standing in the doorway, listening. Then she ran from the room.

"How can she possibly believe that?" Mom asked. "Doesn't she know that I, of all people, sympathize and identify?"

I wasn't sure if Mom was talking to me or to herself.

On Monday afternoon, while I was sitting on our front steps waiting for Paul to give Charles his break, Tarren drove up. She looked very pretty in a summer dress and sandals, her dark hair pulled back, her cheeks flushed. "I have to leave Roddy for a few hours. Can you watch him? Please, Rachel, it's urgent."

"An obstacle?" I asked, looking into her car, where Roddy was napping with his pacifier in his mouth.

Tarren thought that over. "Not exactly," she said. "More of a . . ."

"A what?" I asked.

"Well, I guess you could call it an obstacle. A romantic obstacle." She looked down and fluttered her eyelashes.

"Really?" I said, hoping for more information.

"Rachel, this isn't something I can discuss with you or your mother or anyone else."

Now I was even more curious.

"He's married," Tarren whispered.

"Who is?" I asked.

"My obstacle," she said.

"Oh." Suddenly I felt very uncomfortable.

"He's my professor, at school. We're . . . involved."

Did that mean what I thought it meant?

"I know what your mother would say and I'm not prepared to take her advice," Tarren said. "Because he's wonderful. Even if he is married. Even if it doesn't make any sense. Do you see what I'm saying?"

"I think so."

"Do I have your word, Rachel . . . that you won't say anything about this?"

I nodded.

She hugged me. "Thanks." Then she opened the car door and reached in for Roddy. "Someday I'll cover for you. That's a promise."

"Do you by any chance know Paul Medeiros?" I asked, as she lifted out Roddy.

"No, should I?"

"He's Charles's tutor . . . he's graduating this month."

She handed Roddy to me. "I don't think I know him." She opened the trunk of her car and pulled out Roddy's stroller.

"What time will you be back?" I said.

"Around six, okay? If anyone asks, just say I'm at the library."

As soon as she pulled away, Roddy woke up and started screaming. "It's okay . . . it's okay . . ." I said, patting him. I tried to get his pacifier back into his mouth but he wouldn't take it. Then I offered him a bottle of apple juice, which he knocked out of my hand. Finally I strapped him into his stroller and wheeled him, at top speed, down to the pond. But he still didn't let up.

"Want to see the ducks?" I asked, lifting him out of his stroller. He thrashed around in my arms and screamed even louder.

Stephanie saw us from across the pond and waved. "Ra . . . chel," she called, "what are you doing?"

I didn't answer. It was obvious what I was doing.

In a minute Steph joined us and took Roddy from me. As soon as she did, he grew quiet and looked around. He seemed surprised to see me. Steph talked softly to him. Then she set him down on the ground and he began to crawl toward the pond, stopping along the way to pull up blades of grass that he stuffed into his mouth. We followed, also on hands and knees, making sure he didn't actually swallow anything.

Later, Steph said, "Can I stay over on Saturday night . . . because my mother has a date with the StairMaster and I'm not about to hang around the house waiting to meet him."

"Sure," I said. "Should we ask Alison, too?"

"Yeah, that'd be fun . . . like the old days."

I wanted to ask what she meant by *the old days* but I stopped myself, afraid I might spoil the moment.

THIRTEEN

Dad is a Gemini. His birthday is June 3. According to my book on horoscopes, you can't ever *really* know a Gemini. They have two sides. One you see, one you don't. I guess the side you don't see with Dad is the side that sent him to bed for six weeks after Grandpa died.

Mom left Jess and me a list of things to do for Dad's birthday dinner on Wednesday night. Jess doesn't work at Going Places on Wednesdays. The menu was honey-glazed chicken, wild rice and sugar snaps. Jess and I baked the cake—chocolate with buttercream frosting—while Paul was tutoring Charles. We decorated it with forty-seven candles plus one for good measure.

"Well . . . doesn't this look festive!" Mom said when she got home from work. She admired the table we'd set with our best linens and dishes. We'd even used Gram's silver, which was passed down from *her* mother. It's ornate and very beautiful, but we hardly ever use it because you can't put it in the dishwasher. It goes to the first daughter in the family, so Jess will inherit it someday. Maybe she'll let me borrow it on special occasions.

"What would I do without the two of you?" Mom asked, shaking two Tylenol out of a bottle, then washing them down with a glass of water.

Jessica didn't answer. She's still angry at Mom for listening to Dr. Lucas about not taking Accutane. Her skin looks angry, too—red and broken out, with swellings on her chin and forehead. Tomorrow she's got an appointment to see the dermatologist Rowena recommended.

Mom headed upstairs to get changed, and when she came down a few minutes later, she said, "Rachel . . . get Charles, would you? Dad will be home any minute."

"Charles doesn't eat with us . . . remember?"

"Tonight is a special occasion."

"We'd have a better time without him," I told her.

"Rachel, please! We have to make an effort."

"I don't see why," I muttered under my breath.

"Because that's the way I want it," Mom said, setting another place at the table.

"Okay . . . okay . . ." I said.

Charles's room is painted lipstick red, which was his favorite color when he was thirteen, the year he persuaded Mom and Dad to let him move downstairs. Last year, before he went away to school, he taped an embarrassing poster to the wall behind his bed. It shows a woman wearing only red boots. I WANT YOU! she's saying.

Mom was offended by it but Dad convinced her Charles was entitled to his privacy. So his room was declared off-limits to the rest of us, as long as he kept it reasonably clean. But keeping his room clean has never been a problem for Charles. Jessica is the one who lives in a mess. Charles likes things in order. Once, when I was in fourth grade, I made the mistake of letting Stephanie borrow one of his *Batman* comics, and he almost killed me for taking it out of its plastic wrapper.

Now I knocked on his door and when he called, "Come in . . ." I opened it slowly, not sure of what I might find. The shades were pulled, making it very dark except for a single bulb inside the slide projector. Charles lay on his bed, a black baseball hat on his head. He was munching chips dipped in salsa and swigging Coke from a can as he flipped through a tray of slides with his remote control.

"Look at this picture, Rachel . . ." he said, as if he were expecting me. "Remember when this was taken?"

I turned to look at the screen and saw a picture of the two of us at the lake in New Hampshire, where we go every summer to visit Aunt Joan. I'm about six and Charles is eight. We have a huge fish between us. We're both laughing and pointing to it. We look happy. Were we? I don't remember.

"Mom says your presence is requested at the dinner table," I told him. "We're celebrating Dad's birthday."

He cut off the projector, jumped off the bed, smoothed out his shirt and gave me a smile. "Do I look . . . acceptable?"

I nodded.

When Dad came home, he feigned surprise. "What's this?" he asked, eyeing the festive table.

"Happy birthday!" the rest of us shouted.

We go through this with each of our birthdays. Even though we're never surprised, we always pretend we are. We sit down to dinner before we open presents. Mom started that rule when we were little. Otherwise we'd get too involved in our gifts and forget about the food.

All through dinner Charles didn't make one rude remark. *Not one.* He ate heartily, complimenting us on the food, telling Dad he didn't look a day older than forty-five. He told charming stories about birthday parties he remembered. But I couldn't help noticing there were just three wrapped gifts on the table, not four. And I wondered how Charles would feel when Dad opened something from each of us, but not from him.

After the main course Charles insisted on helping

Jess and me clear the dishes. He even scraped the bread crumbs off the table like a waiter in an elegant restaurant. He asked if there was anything else he could do.

Jessica almost fainted. "I think that's about it," she said, lighting the candles on the cake.

"Wait!" Charles called, as we were about to carry it in. "This is the stuff family memories are made of." While he ran out of the room, trying to find the camera, Jess and I looked at each other. We didn't know what to think.

Charles snapped away on our Polaroid as we sang "Happy Birthday." It took three tries for Dad to get all forty-eight candles out. Then Jess moved the cake to the center of the table and we took our seats to watch Dad open his presents.

Jess gave him a book. She'd showed it to me earlier.

"What do you think?" she'd asked.

"*The Pencil*?" I said, leafing through it, amazed that anyone had written such a book. It was four hundred pages long.

"Look at the subtitle," she said. "*A History of Design and Circumstance.* You know Dad loves anything having to do with history."

And now, as Dad opened it, he seemed really pleased. "I've been meaning to check this out of the library," he told Jess. "Thank you, honey."

I gave Dad a snow globe. Inside is a tiny skier perched on a hill. Dad loves to ski. The second it snows, he straps on his cross-country skis and off he goes, around Palfrey's Pond, through the woods, even on the roads before they're plowed. One winter he got a pair of snowshoes and tried walking to school in them.

Dad turned the snow globe upside down and shook, then watched as snow fell on the little skier. "Thank you, Rachel," Dad said quietly. "I love it. It'll keep me going till next winter."

I knew he really meant it. With Mom it's a lot harder. She doesn't like most things that other people choose for her. That's why Jess and I always decide on something from the two of us. Like the Mother's Day subscription to that magazine. The sample copy is still on her bedside table. I wonder if she's ever actually looked at the pictures inside.

Then Dad opened the final box, from Mom, which held an envelope with two tickets to a concert at Carnegie Hall this coming Saturday night. Music is Dad's thing, not Mom's, but she tries for him. They smiled across the table at each other.

"Well," Mom said, "shall we cut the cake?"

"Wait!" Charles pushed back his chair. "I haven't given Dad my gift yet." He stood up and cleared his throat. "Dad . . ." he began, then paused to clear his throat again. "Dad . . . on this night, on the anniversary of your forty-seventh birthday, I give to you the gift of living history." He paused and looked at each of us. "I give you back your roots." He paused again. "From this night and forevermore . . ."

What was he up to this time?

"From this night," he continued, "I will proudly carry forth the name of our ancestors . . . from this night I will be known as Charles Stefan *Rybczynski*."

There was a deadly silence at the table. And then Jessica blurted out exactly what I was thinking. "You mean you're changing your last name from Robinson to Ryb-something?"

"I'm not changing it, Jess," Charles explained. "I'm reclaiming my true name . . . *our* true name."

Dad had a false smile on his face. "Well . . ." he began.

But Mom interrupted. "Are you contemplating a legal name change?" she asked Charles.

"Mom . . . Mom . . ." Charles shook his head. "Ever the lawyer. Does it really matter whether or not I go through the formalities of changing my name?"

"Yes," Mom said, "it does."

Charles pulled a document out of his back pocket and unfolded it carefully. He spread it out in front of Dad. "I'll need your signature," he said, "since I'm under eighteen. But I told my lawyer that wouldn't be a problem."

"Your lawyer?" Mom asked.

"Yes," Charles said. "My lawyer . . . Henry Simon."

"You went to see Henry without discussing it with us?" Henry Simon is an old family friend. He went to law school with Mom and Dad. He practices in town.

"Don't worry," Charles said. "I set up an appointment. I wore a nice shirt."

"You had no—" Mom began.

"I explained it was a surprise," Charles said. "And Henry . . . Mr. Simon, that is . . . promised he wouldn't say anything. He didn't, did he?"

"No," Mom said. "I wish he had."

"Poor Mom," Charles said. "You're feeling left out, aren't you? But you can do it, too. You can become *Judge Rybczynski*. It's easy." He looked around the table. "You can all become *Rybczynskis*."

"No thanks!" Jess said. "Can you imagine your children trying to print that name in first grade?"

I laughed. I couldn't help myself.

"Let's not get ahead of ourselves," Charles said, which made Dad laugh, too.

"Well, Charles . . ." Dad finally said, "it's a mouthful to say and a bitch to spell. . . ."

Charles handed him a pen, but before Dad could sign his name Mom said, "Victor . . . don't you think you should sleep on it?"

"What for?" Dad asked. "If Charles wants the family name, it's his." Dad signed his name to the document, then sat back in his seat. "You know . . . .I remember my grandfather telling me a story about the day he got to Ellis Island. The officials couldn't say his name, let alone spell it. My grandparents didn't speak a word of English but they understood what was happening. And they were all for it. A new country. A new life. A new name. I wonder what they'd think if they were here tonight?"

"I think they'd be honored," Charles said.

"You could be right," Dad told him.

Mom picked up the cake knife. "I guess it's time for dessert," she said, cutting into the cake as if she were trying to kill it.

Later I overheard Mom and Dad in the kitchen. "We're talking about a name that's going to follow him the rest of his life," Mom said.

"Maybe . . . maybe not," Dad told her. "And either way I still think it was better to sign, without making it into a production."

"You actually *like* the idea, don't you?"

"There's a certain strength to a name like that," Dad admitted.

"Well, I hate the whole thing! It's just one more way for him to separate himself from the rest of the family."

"He's testing us . . . you know that."

"I'm tired of being tested!" Mom said. "I'm tired

of him manipulating us. And I hate what this is doing to the girls."

I stood with my back against the wall right outside the kitchen. My heart was thumping so loud I was sure they could hear it.

"Sometimes I feel . . ." Mom continued. "Sometimes I feel such anger toward him I scare myself. Then I remember what a sweet, clever baby he was." Her voice broke. "If I didn't have those memories to fall back on, I don't think I could tolerate another day of his mischief."

"Nell . . . honey . . ."

I sneaked a look into the kitchen. Dad was holding Mom in his arms. I backed away as quietly as possible, right into Charles, who jabbed me in the sides with his fingers, making me cry out.

"What?" Dad asked, rushing into the hall.

"Nothing," I said.

Charles laughed. "Rachel's very edgy," he said. "She's worried she won't be able to spell my last name."

FOURTEEN

How do you *spell* that name?" Stephanie said. She and Alison had come over to spend Saturday night.

"R-y-b-c-z-y-n-s-k-i."

"How do you pronounce it again?" Alison asked, unrolling her sleeping bag and placing it next to Steph's.

"Rib-jin-ski," I told her.

"That's an incredible name," Alison said.

"Why would anyone *want* such a long last name?" Steph said. She pulled a stuffed coyote out of her overnight bag. She's slept with that coyote since her father won it for her at a carnival. She says she plans to take it to college with her. She says she plans to take it on her honeymoon if and when she decides to get married.

"You'd have to ask Charles," I told her.

"Where is he?"

"Stephanie!" I said. "Don't you dare ask him!"

"But you said . . ."

"She was just kidding," Alison told Steph. "Right, Rachel?"

"I was definitely not serious!" I said.

"Is Charles home?" Alison asked.

"I believe he's in his room."

Mom and Dad had left for New York on the 4:30 train. They planned to have dinner at their favorite restaurant before the birthday concert at Carnegie Hall. Mom wore her slinky black dress, the one Jessica *borrowed* for her junior prom. Jess got home from work before they left. "How come you're so dressed up?" she'd asked when she saw Mom.

"It's a benefit," Mom told her, "for the Legal Defense Fund. There's a party after the concert."

Jess seemed nervous, especially when Mom looked in the mirror and said, "I don't know. There's something about this dress. Does it look odd to you, Victor?"

"It looks great!" Dad said. Obviously no one had told him what Jess wore to the prom.

Mom sniffed herself. "It doesn't smell like my perfume," she said.

"Whose could it possibly be?" Jessica asked, sounding defensive.

"I've no idea," Mom said. "Something just doesn't feel right."

"It shouldn't feel any different than it always feels," Jessica said. I shot her a look, hoping she'd shut up about Mom's dress, but she didn't. "It shouldn't feel any different than when you wore it to that benefit for the homeless."

"Maybe I've gained weight," Mom said, adjusting the straps.

"You never gain weight," Jess told her. "It's probably that you're not wearing those dangling earrings." Jess was talking about the earrings *she* wore to the prom.

"They'd be too much for tonight," Mom said.

When Mom and Dad finally left, Jessica let out a long sigh. "Do you think she guessed?" Jess asked.

"No, but you were acting so guilty she would have in another minute."

"I couldn't help myself," she said. "I didn't mean to say anything but the words just kept pouring out. I should have taken the dress to the cleaners."

"Mom'll probably send it after tonight. Stop worrying."

Jess looked at me and laughed. "This must be a first . . . *you* telling *me* not to worry!"

Later Jess went out with Kristen and Richie. Ed and Marcy have the flu.

A few minutes before seven, the three of us took our positions at the windows in my room facing Steph's house. Even though Steph refuses to meet the StairMaster, she is very curious about him.

At five after seven, a red pickup truck pulled up to Steph's. A guy in jeans and a leather jacket got out. A guy with a ponytail. Stephanie inhaled sharply.

"It's probably just a delivery," Alison told her.

We watched him swagger up to the front door. He wasn't carrying a package. In fact, his hands were in his pockets until he rang the bell. Mrs. Hirsch answered.

"He's probably selling magazines," Alison said.

Steph didn't say anything.

Mrs. Hirsch was wearing jeans, western boots and a fringed jacket. She linked her arm through his. They laughed as they got into his truck.

"I guess he's not selling magazines," Alison said.

"I can't believe this!" Steph finally said. "How old do you think he is?"

"Over eighteen," Alison said.

"Probably thirty," I said.

"Right," Alison said, glancing at me. "And they're probably just friends. Younger men and older women make good friends for each other. I read about it in *People* magazine."

But Stephanie wasn't listening. "And with a ponytail!" she said. "This is so embarrassing!"

If I were a Natural Helper right now, what would I do? I reminded myself of the first steps we learned at the introductory meeting. *Listen, not just to the spoken but to the unspoken. Be aware of body language.* Right now Steph had her arms folded across her chest. An angry pose, a defiant one. *Be on her side. Offer encouragement and support, but not advice . . .*

But as soon as the red truck pulled out, Steph said, "Let's play Spit!" You could tell she didn't want to talk about her mother and the StairMaster.

So for the next hour we played Spit, a card game Alison had taught us. It's meant for just two players but we've invented a way it can be played with three. I used to hate it, but lately I've learned it's an excellent way to relieve tension. It's such a fast game you can't afford the time to think—you just have to react. And it's so silly we always wind up laughing our heads off and singing "Side by Side," our theme song.

Tonight, when we got to the section that goes

Through all kinds of weather
What if the sky should fall . . .

Stephanie stopped and turned to me. "That's the perfect line for you, Rachel."

"What line?" I asked.

"That line." She sang it. "What if the sky should fall?"

"I don't know what you mean," I told her.

"You always think the sky is falling."

"I do not think the sky is falling."

"You think the worst is going to happen," she said. "And that's the same thing."

"I do not think the worst is *necessarily* going to happen!"

Alison held up her hands. "Let's not get into one of these stupid arguments," she said. "Okay?"

"Who's arguing?" I asked.

"I didn't mean it was bad or anything," Steph said. "I just meant . . ."

But we were interrupted by a sudden blast of music. When I opened my bedroom door, it grew even louder. I walked to the stairway and called downstairs, "Kindly lower the volume!" My choice of words made Alison and Stephanie laugh.

But Charles either couldn't hear me or chose to ignore my request. Now the neighbors would start calling. There are rules at Palfrey's Pond and one of them is no noise loud enough to break the tranquillity of the area. I love that word, *tranquillity*. It means peacefulness, serenity.

I looked at Stephanie and Alison. "I better go tell him to turn it down." As they followed me, the phone rang. "I knew it," I said. "Neighbors."

"Aren't you going to answer?" Steph asked.

"No," I said. "Let the machine take the message."

We paused outside Charles's bedroom door. The sound of the music was deafening. "Metallica," Alison said to Steph. They know the names of all the groups. But they don't know Bach from Beethoven.

Finally I knocked. No response. So I banged on his door with two fists and shouted, "Charles . . . turn that down!"

Suddenly the music clicked off and the door opened, just enough for Charles to have a look. Stephanie and Alison giggled nervously. They find anything having to do with Charles exciting.

"The neighbors are going to call to complain!" I told him.

"It's my warden," Charles announced. As he opened his door all the way, a pungent odor hit us. It was so dark and smoky in his room, it took me a minute to realize he wasn't alone.

Marcella, the eighth-grade slut, sat on the floor with Adrienne, a ninth grader who has a major attitude. There were also two guys I'd never seen before, swigging beer from bottles. And over in the corner, looking unhappy and out of place, were Dana Carpenter and Jeremy Dragon! What were *they* doing here?

"Macbeth!" Jeremy said when he saw me. "What are *you* doing here?"

"I live here," I told him. Why would Jeremy and Dana be at a party in Charles's room, especially since everyone knows about their fight over Marcella?

"You live here?" he asked, surprised.

"This is my baby sister," Charles said. "Rachel Lowilla, the child prodigy." He grabbed my wrist.

"Come in, Rachel . . ." He beckoned to Stephanie and Alison. "Come in, girls. We're celebrating my name change. Have a beer . . . have a joint . . . loosen up!"

"No thank you!" As I tried to pull away, Dana came up behind him and rested her hand on his arm. "Charles," she said quietly.

Charles let go of me and wrapped an arm around Dana's waist. They smiled at each other. What was going on here? "You're going to read about my little sister someday," Charles told his guests. "In addition to developing a vaccine to prevent hair balls in lions, she's going to—"

"Murder her brother!" I shouted, not waiting for him to finish. Then I slammed the door and broke for the stairs, with Alison and Steph following. When we got back to my room, I slammed *my* door and woke the cats.

"I *knew* Dana liked Charles!" Steph said, flopping in my chair.

"Some people have no taste," I muttered.

"And *he* likes her!" Steph continued.

"I thought he liked me," Alison said.

Steph and I looked at her.

"Well, he acted like he did . . . didn't he?" she asked. "I mean, that night I came over to get a book, he definitely acted like he was interested. You were there, Rachel."

I shrugged.

Alison continued, "I think what happened is he realized I'm just in seventh grade and he decided I'm too young . . . for now."

"Right," Steph said. She waited for me to agree.

There was no point in hurting Alison, so I said, "It's possible."

"Anything's possible," Alison said, using one of my favorite lines.

"Right," Steph and I said at the same time.

We were quiet for a minute, until we heard a voice calling, "Macbeth . . . where are you, Macbeth?"

Jeremy Dragon?

"Open the door," Steph whispered.

I opened it.

"Hey . . ." Jeremy said.

"Hey . . ." I said back. *I could not believe this!*

"Aren't you going to invite me in?" he asked. I stepped aside. He walked into my room and looked around. "Nice," he said. "Very . . . neat."

"Yeah," Steph said, "a hot Saturday night for Rachel is folding her socks!" Then she laughed nervously.

I could have killed her!

But Jeremy thought it was a joke. He laughed and said, "So, is that what you're doing . . . folding Macbeth's socks?"

Steph said, "No . . . we're just hanging out."

"Well, if you're just hanging out," Jeremy said, "how about a game?"

"A game?" I repeated.

"Yeah, a game . . . like Monopoly."

"You want to play Monopoly?" I asked. *I definitely could not believe this!*

"Yeah," he said. "That is, I wouldn't mind."

I looked at Alison and Steph. We were having trouble keeping straight faces. I went to my closet, reached up to my top shelf and pulled down my Monopoly set, which Tarren had given to me when I was in third grade.

The four of us settled on the floor, with Jeremy seated between me and Steph, across from Alison. He chose the little race car for his token. I took the hat.

We rolled to see who would start. Alison got the high number. None of us asked Jeremy anything about Charles's party. And he didn't volunteer any information. For the next two hours we concentrated on Monopoly. Midway through the game I went down to the kitchen and brought up a bottle of apple juice, a bag of pretzels, and a tin of cookies my aunt had sent us. Jeremy ate three-quarters of the cookies and drank half the juice.

The game finally ended when Alison built hotels on Boardwalk and Park Place and the rest of us went bankrupt. By then it was close to eleven and the three of us walked Jeremy downstairs. He didn't head for Charles's room or even call good-night to anyone at the party, which, from the sound of it, was still going strong.

I didn't want to think about Charles's party. I'm not the family warden, despite what Charles says. It's not my job to report on him to my parents. If he does something that directly affects me, that's different. If not, let them find out on their own.

"Good-night, Macbeth," Jeremy said as he went out the door and down the path. "Good game."

The three of us went back up to my room and fell across my bed, laughing hysterically. Then we were absolutely quiet. Then we began laughing hysterically again, until our sides were splitting.

I woke up sometime later to see Stephanie sitting in the window. I crept out of bed and kneeled beside her. The StairMaster's truck was parked in front of her house. "It's been there for an hour at least," she whispered. "And don't tell me they're just talking."

"It is possible."

"Please!"

"Sorry."

"I hate this!" Steph whispered, looking over at Alison, who was totally out of it in her sleeping bag. "It's so . . . disgusting!"

I nodded.

She choked up. "If she marries someone like him, I'm moving out. I'll go live with my dad."

"You can live with us," I said.

She smiled. "Thanks."

I put my arm around her shoulder. "It must be really hard to see your mother with someone like him."

"It is . . . it's so hard." Then she cried. I held her and patted her back. "Thank you," she said after a few minutes. "I think I'll go to sleep now."

I wish I could just let go and cry like that. I wish I knew how to let my friends comfort me.

FIFTEEN

At the bus stop on Monday morning, Dana said, "Just so you know . . . it's all over between Jeremy and me."

"You don't have to explain," I told her.

"But I want to. You seemed so . . ." She paused, trying to find the right word. "You seemed so *surprised* the other night."

"I was."

"You really don't know Charles, do you?" she said. "If you'd just give him half a chance, you might be . . ." She paused again, then came up with the same word. "*Surprised*."

"He's a very surprising person," I agreed.

She shook her head at me, obviously annoyed. "I really don't understand you, Rachel. Most of the time you seem so grown-up, and then you . . ."

I glanced over at Alison and Stephanie, who were listening to every word.

"I just hope you'll try to get to know your brother," Dana continued, "because he's a very warm and intelligent person."

"If you say so."

"And would you, please, stop acting like such a bitch!" With that, she turned and marched away from me in a huff.

Now Stephanie and Alison were really cracking up. I went over to them, took each one by the arm like a mother with two small children, and led them away.

"Is she *really* going with Charles?" Alison asked.

"It sounds like *she* thinks so," Steph said.

"What about *him*?" Alison asked. "Does *he* think he's going with *her*?"

"I wouldn't know," I said. "Charles and I haven't exchanged a word since Saturday night."

That afternoon Dana rang our doorbell. "I'm here to see Charles," she said when I came to the door.

"Charles is with his tutor," I told her. "He's busy until five-thirty."

"I know that," she said, as if she knows everything about our family. "But they take a break at four-thirty, don't they?"

"Yes," I said, "but just for ten minutes."

She checked her watch. It was quarter after four. "If you don't mind, I'll wait."

"Suit yourself," I told her. But I didn't invite her inside.

"And Rachel," she said, "I'd really appreciate it if you wouldn't discuss this with Jeremy again."

"Discuss what with Jeremy?" I asked, since I've never actually discussed anything with him.

"*This*," Dana said, as if I were stupid. "Charles and me."

"I've never discussed you and my brother with Jeremy."

"Oh, please!" she said. "It's not like I didn't see the two of you coming out of math class today."

But what Jeremy had said on the way out of math class today had nothing to do with Dana.

He'd said, "I can't say I like your brother, Macbeth."

"I can't say I do, either," I'd answered.

"He's too full of himself."

"He's definitely full of something."

"He's not . . . you know . . . as *real* as you," he'd said, looking directly into my eyes. The way he said it made it sound like a compliment, but I couldn't be sure.

So Dana sat on the front steps to wait for Charles. Burt rubbed against her leg and she petted him, cooing, "Good kitty . . . sweet kitty." I turned away and went back into the house.

At four-thirty, when Charles and Paul came into the kitchen for their break, Charles asked, "Is Dana here?"

"Out front," I told him.

"You could have invited her in," he said.

"You didn't mention you were expecting company," I answered.

Paul dropped an arm around Charles's shoulder and said, "No distractions during our time together. Ask her to come back at five-thirty . . . okay?"

"Okay," Charles called, on his way to the front door. He didn't sound angry or even annoyed. I don't understand how Charles can get along so well with Paul but not with any of us. If Mom or Dad had said no distractions during tutoring, Charles would have told them where to go. But with Paul, he's a totally different person. He's keeping up with his schoolwork and even moving ahead of where he would be if he were just finishing ninth grade. Of course since he's already finished ninth grade once before, that's not surprising. But still . . . As soon as Charles left the kitchen, Paul looked at me and said, "What about you, Rachel?"

"*What* about me?" I asked.

"Do you have a boyfriend?"

"No!" I answered too quickly, feeling my lower lip begin to twitch. I couldn't look at him. Instead I said, "I have to practice now. Excuse me." And I ran from the room.

"When am I going to hear you play?" Paul called after me.

"Whenever . . ." I called back.

I wish I could let Paul know how I feel about him.

I often imagine us having deep, meaningful conversations. I often imagine us kissing passionately. Sometimes I imagine *more* than kisses. If Steph knew what I was thinking, she'd be relieved. She'd say, *So you're normal after all . . . at least in* that *way!* But she can't know. No one can. Paul has to remain my secret.

SIXTEEN

Mom lost her big jury trial on the same day I won a major debate against a ninth grader at Kennedy Junior High. Toad Scrudato, the only other seventh grader on our team, said, "Rachel, you were brilliant!" Those were his exact words. So obviously I was feeling pretty good. This was before I found out about Mom. At the time I didn't even mind that Toad's father's car broke down on the Merritt Parkway on the way home from the debate and we had to be towed to a garage, then wait an hour while a new battery was installed.

I called home at quarter to six to say I'd be late. Charles answered. I asked for Dad. He said Dad was coaching at a track meet. When I asked for Mom, he said she wasn't home yet, either. "And neither is Jessica, so that leaves me, Rachel. Do you have a message for me?" I told him about Mr. Scrudato's car but nothing else.

Then Toad and I sat on the curb outside the garage and read while Mr. Scrudato made call after call on his car phone. Toad and I have known each other since kindergarten. We're sort of an odd couple. He's always been the smallest kid in our class and I've always been the tallest, until Max Wilson moved here. But we have a lot in common intellectually.

By the time Toad's father dropped me off at our house, it was after seven. As soon as I walked in, Dad took me aside and said, "Mom lost her case. She's pretty upset."

"Should I say something?"

Dad shook his head. "You know how she is. She doesn't want to talk about it."

The same way I was when I missed *sesquipedalian* and lost the state spelling championship last year.

Still, I was surprised when Mom didn't come to dinner. It's not as if this is the first case she's ever lost.

"She's just disappointed," Dad told Jess and me as he grilled hamburgers on the patio. "She wanted to go out on a high note."

"Who?" Jess asked, as if she lived on another planet.

"Mom," Dad said. "This is a blow to her pride but she'll get over it." He sounded like he was trying to convince not only us, but himself. I must have looked strange because Dad reached out to touch my arm. "Don't worry, Rachel . . ."

Until then I wasn't worried.

Charles passed by, grabbing a roll. He flipped a

hamburger onto it and smothered it with salsa. "Is it true?" he asked, taking a huge bite. "Did the perfect litigator really lose her final case?"

Dad snapped at him. "A little compassion is in order this evening, Charles!"

"Yeah, sure," he said, with a mouthful. "I've got compassion. I'm just saying, you know, we'd all be better off if we were less competitive."

"Speak for yourself," I said.

"I always speak for myself, Rachel," he said, going out through the patio gate.

After dinner I went upstairs. The door to Mom and Dad's bedroom was open a crack. I knocked lightly. "Mom . . ." No answer. I pushed the door open and tiptoed in. She was asleep with an ice pack across her forehead. I looked around and was surprised to see her suit tossed over a chair and her shoes in the middle of the floor as if she'd kicked them off on her way into bed. "I'm sorry you lost your case," I whispered as I picked them up and put them in her closet. But she didn't hear me.

I went down the hall to my room and sat at my desk, staring out the window. I wasn't in the mood for my math homework. I wondered what my teacher would do if I came in tomorrow and used that as an excuse. *Sorry, I didn't feel like doing my homework last night.* She'd probably call Mrs. Balaban, who would send me to Dr. Sparks!

While I was sitting there, Dad came in. "Tell me about the debate."

I didn't want to talk about it now. It didn't seem right to be happy about winning when Mom was so unhappy. So I just gave him the basics.

"I'm proud of you, honey," he said. "But I'd love you just the same if you'd lost today. You know that, don't you?"

"Why do you always say that?"

"Say what?"

"That you'd love me just the same if I lost."

"Because it's true."

"That's not what I mean."

"Then what?"

I wasn't sure how to explain it. "I mean," I said, trying to find the right words, "why can't you just accept good news?"

"I guess I want you to remember that winning's not the most important thing in life."

"But it's a lot better than losing," I told him. "Just ask Mom."

He ran his hands through his hair. He does that when he's thinking. So I quickly added, "Mom would be glad I won. I don't see why you can't be, too."

"I *am* glad, Rachel. I just want you to keep it in perspective." He dropped a kiss on top of my head. "I've got to run over to the library. Be back in an hour."

When he was gone, I jotted down *Keep it in per-*

spective on my math worksheet. Under that I wrote
Victor Robinson, Tuesday, June 9.

The next afternoon, right before school ended, I was
called to Mr. Herman's office. The one time in my
entire life I didn't do my homework and I've been
reported to the vice principal! I felt sick. I wondered if
this would go down on my permanent record. When
I got to his office, Toad was there, too, looking as ter-
rified as me. Mr. Herman told us to make ourselves
comfortable but neither of us moved an inch. Even
though he has a friendly smile, Mr. Herman's size
makes him formidable. Kids call him the sumo
wrestler.

"Good news," he said. "You've both been recommended for Challenge, a new program for junior
high students who excel academically. If your parents
give permission, you'll be taking courses in math and
science at the college next year."

As he explained it to us, I began to feel like I
couldn't breathe. Another program to separate me
from my friends! When he asked if we had any questions, I managed to say, "Do we *have* to?"

"Have to what, Rachel?"

"Do this?"

Toad looked at me as if I were totally insane. But
I didn't care. I felt light-headed and grabbed hold of
the back of a chair facing Mr. Herman's desk.

"It's entirely up to you," he said. "It's an honor just to be asked."

"A person can't do everything just because she's asked," I told him.

"A good point," he said.

I definitely could not breathe! I closed my eyes and forced myself to count backward from one hundred.

Mr. Herman never noticed. He went right on talking. "Well, I guess this has really caught both of you by surprise!" When neither of us responded, he cleared his throat. "Here's a letter to take home to your parents." He handed one to Toad and another to me. "Think of this as an opportunity not to be missed."

As the bell rang, I shoved the letter into my purse. I wish I could explain to Mr. Herman and everyone else that right now I don't *need* another opportunity.

On the bus home from school Alison said, "Are you okay, Rachel?"

"Yes . . . why?"

"You look sort of pale."

Steph squinted at me. "No, she doesn't. She's always that color."

"She's usually got *some* pink in her cheeks," Alison said. "Maybe she's coming down with that flu."

"She looks fine to me," Steph said.

While they were arguing, some guy shoved Jeremy

Dragon, who was getting off at the next stop, right into my lap.

"Sorry about that, Macbeth," he said as he pulled himself up.

I could feel my cheeks burning, especially when the driver yelled at us to quit fooling around.

As Jeremy got off the bus, Alison whispered, "You're not pale anymore, Rachel!"

"I wish he'd fall onto me!" Steph said, making all three of us laugh.

The minute I got home, I folded and refolded the letter from Mr. Herman until it was small enough to fit into the secret compartment of my favorite box. Since Mr. Herman says participating in Challenge is entirely up to me, I don't have to show it to my parents. At least not yet.

SEVENTEEN

Jessica's been taking Accutane for a week. The doctor Rowena recommended told Jess about the possible side effects and gave her a booklet to read. But Jess decided to try it, anyway. I don't blame her. I'd try anything if I had her kind of cystic acne. Before the doctor gave her the prescription Jess had to sign a paper stating she would not get pregnant, because if you take Accutane while you are, it causes serious birth defects. As if Jess would be foolish enough to get pregnant even if she had a boyfriend, which she doesn't.

Jess will have to see the doctor once a month for twenty weeks. She'll need blood tests to make sure everything's going okay. She says Accutane can take up to four months to work but some patients see a difference right away. I hope she'll be one of them.

Tarren and Roddy came over for dinner on Thursday night. Tarren took one look at Jess and said, "Your skin looks . . . painful."

"Well, it's not as painful as acne," Jess told her. Her face was totally dried out and peeling. So far Jessica's only side effects are dry eyes and cracked lips. She carries a tube of medicated lip gloss with her and has to put drops in her eyes twice a day.

Before we sat down to dinner, Tarren cornered me. "Listen, Rachel . . ." she said, shifting Roddy from one hip to the other, "I wanted to thank you for that day you watched Roddy."

I nodded. "How's it going with your romantic obstacle?"

"It's going great."

I nodded again, then looked around to make sure no one was within earshot. "Have you by any chance met Paul Medeiros?" I spoke very softly. "He's a history major at the school of education."

"You've asked me about him before, haven't you?"

"I thought maybe you've met him since then."

Tarren shook her head. "Is he someone special?"

"No," I said quickly, hoping Tarren wouldn't become suspicious. "I mean, he's Charles's tutor . . . and I'm curious . . . but other than that . . ."

"Well, I don't think I know him. Do you want me to ask around?"

"No . . . forget it . . . it's nothing."

"You're sure . . . because I owe you a favor."

"I'm sure," I told her.

Charles joined us for dinner. I don't know why. He hasn't had a meal with us since Dad's birthday. He sat next to Roddy, who was in a Sassy Seat, which attached to the table.

We were having corkscrew pasta with vegetables and Mom's special lemon-and-herb sauce. The green peppers weren't cooked quite enough for me, so I moved them to the side of my plate. Tarren did the same with her mushrooms.

"Tarren," Mom said, "I'd like you to come to my swearing-in ceremony. It's the morning of June twenty-third, in Hartford. After, we'll all go out to lunch."

"Oh, Aunt Nell," Tarren gushed. "I'm honored."

I wondered how long it would take to drive to Hartford. If it's more than half an hour, maybe I can take the train. I wouldn't want to get carsick on the day Mom is sworn in as a judge.

Charles was quiet, intrigued by Roddy, who was slowly and methodically eating Cheerios. He picked up one at a time, using two fingers, brought it to his mouth, got it inside, then mashed it with his gums. He still doesn't have teeth. Tarren says he will soon.

"Was it always your goal to become a judge, Aunt Nell?" Tarren asked, as Dad served the salad.

"I really hadn't given the possibility much thought

until recently," Mom said. "But frankly, after this week, I'm beginning to think it will be a relief."

"What do you mean?" Tarren asked, wide-eyed.

"I lost a case," Mom told her. "I lost my final jury trial." She sounded wistful, almost emotional. This was the first time she'd mentioned the verdict.

"I can't imagine you losing a case!" Tarren said.

"Well, I did," Mom told her, "and I took it personally, even though I know better." She kind of sighed as she speared a tomato. "But I did my best and that's what counts."

Tarren had tears in her eyes. "That is just so moving, Aunt Nell. To know you've done your best even when you've failed."

Charles looked up, suddenly interested. Then Mom said, "I didn't exactly fail, Tarren. I lost a case that I'd rather have won, that's all. It happens." She sounded sure of herself again, like Mom.

"It's all about goals, isn't it?" Tarren asked. "In our Life Studies class we had to write down where we hope to be five years from today, then ten, then twenty. It really got me thinking."

Charles looked over at Tarren. Before he had the chance to pounce, Dad said, "What *are* your goals, Tarren?"

"Well, some of them are personal," Tarren said, with a glance in my direction, "and I'd rather not discuss them. But my professional goal is to become the best fourth-grade teacher I possibly can. To make a difference in a few children's lives."

Charles let out a snort.

Tarren leaned forward in her seat so she could look directly at Charles. "It would be a good course for you to take," she told him. "Talk about someone who needs to clarify his goals!"

Didn't she know better than to start in with him?

"My goals in life are very simple," Charles told her. We all waited for more but first Charles reached for his water glass and took a long drink. Then he wiped his mouth with his napkin. With Charles, timing is everything. Finally he said, "My main goal in life is to be Batman!"

"Really, Charles!" Mom said, as Charles lifted Roddy out of his Sassy Seat and bounced him on his lap to the theme from the Batman movie.

Roddy laughed and said, "Da da . . ."

"I'm not your da da," Charles said, "but speaking of your da da, is he still soaring?"

Tarren sucked in her breath. "As far as I know Bill is still hang gliding, if that's what you mean. We have almost no contact."

"Poor little guy!" Charles patted Roddy's head.

"He doesn't need your pity!" Tarren told Charles. "He's going to be just fine."

"That's the spirit!" Mom said, squeezing Tarren's shoulder.

"Having a runaway father is just one obstacle in his life," Tarren said. "And we all have our obstacles."

"Yeah, look at me," Charles said. "I'm surrounded by mine. My father, the *wimp* . . . my mother, the *ice queen* . . . my big sister, the *potato head* . . . and my little sis—"

Before he had the chance to finish, Jessica pushed back her chair. "I hate you!" she hissed.

"I know that, Jess . . . but you'll get over it."

Mom jumped up, her face purple with rage. "You want to hurt us, Charles? Okay, we're hurt! You want to cause pain? Fine, you have! You want to disrupt the family? Congratulations, you've succeeded!" She banged her fist on the table so hard the dishes rattled.

Roddy began to cry. Tarren snatched him from Charles's lap and whisked him into the kitchen, where his screams grew louder. By then Dad was out of his seat, grabbing hold of Mom, who had lunged at Charles, shouting, "Enough is enough!" A glass she'd knocked over rolled to the edge of the table, tumbled to the floor and smashed.

Charles folded his napkin. "Well," he said, "this pleasant evening seems to be drawing to a close."

As he began to get up from the table, Dad pushed him down again. "Stay right where you are!"

Charles looked surprised for a minute. The color drained from his face. He didn't move.

"We're not going to tolerate any more nights like this!" Dad shouted. "It's time for you to get your act together. Do you understand what I'm saying?"

Mom stood next to Dad, waiting for an answer.

Charles gave them a long look, then asked, "Is that it? Are you finished?"

"Oh, for God's sake!" Mom said, and I could feel her frustration.

"No, I'm not finished," Dad told him. "I'm waiting for you to answer the question!"

"I believe I get your point," Charles said quietly. "Now, may I please be excused?"

Dad didn't answer right away. When he did, his voice was flat. "You're excused to help clean up."

"Thank you." Charles stood, stacked the dinner dishes and carried them into the kitchen.

I ducked under the table to pick up the broken glass.

"I've had it," Mom said to Dad. "This time I have *really* had it."

"We can't give up on him, Nell."

"I'm not saying we should give up on him. I'm saying he's pushed me to the limit!"

Before I'd collected all the glass, the phone rang. "It's Stephanie, Rachel," Tarren called from the kitchen.

"Tell her I can't talk now," I said quietly, from the floor. "Tell her I'll call back."

But I didn't call Stephanie that night. And later, as I lay in bed watching the clock, I played the dinner table scene over and over in my mind, angry at myself for just swallowing everything I was thinking and feeling—for just sitting there, totally paralyzed, waiting to hear what Charles would say about me, almost disappointed that Jess stopped him before he'd had the chance to finish.

I got out of bed and crept down the hall to Jessica's room. But she was sound asleep, breathing evenly. How could she sleep after tonight? How could anyone?

My stomach was killing me. I needed something to soothe it. I moved silently downstairs with Harry right behind me. When I got to the kitchen, I flicked on the light switch and almost keeled over when I saw Charles perched on the counter, gnawing a chicken leg.

"Want a bite?" he asked, holding it out.

"You just about scared me to death!" I told him, keeping my voice low. The last thing I wanted was to wake Mom and Dad. "Why are you in here in the dark?"

"Is there a family rule against conserving energy?"

I didn't answer. Instead I filled the kettle and turned on the burner.

Charles jumped down from the counter. He opened the refrigerator, pulled out the grape juice and held it up, as if to toast me. "Here's to you, Rachel Robinson!" He swigged some juice right out of the bottle, then slammed the door. "Here's to my whole fucking family!"

"You better not let Mom and Dad hear you say that."

"Yeah, right. They'd call the language police. And the language police will drag me to the dictionary to find a more acceptable word for my family, like noble . . . like self-sacrificing . . . like—"

"You were despicable tonight!"

"Thanks, Rachel."

"Why'd you have to hurt everyone? What was the point?"

"The point was to get at the truth."

"Well, you didn't!" I told him. "You didn't even come close."

"Really."

"Yes, really! Mom's not an ice queen."

"Maybe not to you. After all, you're her clone."

"I'm not anybody's clone! And Dad's not a wimp, either."

"Then how come he went to bed for six weeks when Grandpa died? How come he couldn't make it in the real world? How come he gives the Ice Queen all the power?"

"He went to bed when Grandpa died because he was sad."

"Oh, that's sweet, Rachel. But plenty of people get

sad and they don't climb into bed and pull the covers over their heads for six weeks!"

"He wasn't happy being a lawyer, so he quit. What's wrong with that?" I paused for a moment. "And Mom doesn't have all the power. He's the one who's always stopping her."

"Right . . . because he's a wimp! He'll do anything to avoid confrontation!"

"He didn't avoid it tonight, did he? He told you off and so did Mom!"

"You call that telling me off?" He smirked. "I call that pathetic."

"Mom and Dad are *not* pathetic!"

"Are we talking about the same Mom and Dad? The Nell and Victor with the bedroom upstairs at the end of the hall?"

"I'm talking about *my* parents. I don't know about yours!"

"When are you going to face the facts, Rachel? This is a very screwed-up family!"

"You're the part that's screwed up."

"I don't deny it. But the rest of you . . ." He stopped and shook his head.

"All families have problems," I said, thinking of Steph and how angry she is at her mother for dating the StairMaster.

He laughed. " 'Happy families are all alike; every unhappy family is unhappy in its own way.' "

That sounded familiar but I couldn't remember where I'd heard it.

Charles laughed again. "Tolstoy, Rachel. Don't tell me you haven't read him yet?"

"I plan to . . . this summer."

"I certainly hope so. I wouldn't want you to fall behind. After all, you've got to be the best."

"I like being the best!"

"What happens when you find out it's not always possible?"

"I've already found out and I'm surviving!"

He paused, as if I'd caught him by surprise. "You know something, Rachel, you've got possibilities. With a little coaching . . ."

"I don't need any coaching from you!" I told him. "I'm figuring out life by myself, thank you."

"Whatever you say, little sister." He started to walk away.

I called, "What do you want from us, Charles?"

He spun around. "What do I want?" He looked up, as if he'd find the answer on the ceiling. Then he repeated the question, quietly, to himself. "What do I want . . . ?"

I waited, but for once Charles seemed at a loss for words.

EIGHTEEN

The next night Charles didn't come to dinner. I wasn't surprised. But even without him at the table, it's become so tense it's hard to eat. The rest of us didn't have much to say until Dad announced we're going to see a family counselor, someone named Dr. Michael Embers.

"I don't see why *we* have to go to a counselor!" Jessica cried, with a nod in my direction. "There's nothing *wrong* with Rachel and me!"

"Because it's *family* therapy," Dad told her, sounding weary.

"But *Charles* is the one with the problem!" Jess argued, which is exactly what I was thinking.

Dad shoved his plate out of the way. "Please don't make this more difficult than it already is." He reached into his pocket and pulled out a packet of Pepto-Bismol tablets. He popped two into his mouth and chewed them up slowly. He looked very tired. So did Mom. I really and truly resent Charles for making them so unhappy.

"Well," Jessica said, "if we *have* to go, I don't see why we can't see a woman!"

"According to *some* people," Mom said, "there are already too many authoritarian women in Charles's life."

Does that mean us? I wondered, looking at Jessica. What a joke! Charles walks all over us. We have no authority over him!

On Monday night at six, we went to Dr. Embers's office. He shook hands with each of us, but only Charles introduced himself using two names. "Charles Rybczynski," he said. If Dr. Embers noticed Charles had a different last name, he didn't show it.

He said, "Please, sit down . . . make yourselves comfortable."

His office was arranged like a living room, with a small sofa, two armchairs, a wooden rocker and a couple of other chairs. I sat stiffly in one of the armchairs, next to Jessica, who sat in the other. Mom and Dad shared the sofa, and Charles settled in the rocker.

Dr. Embers was younger than I'd expected, with wiry light hair, washed-out blue eyes and a runner's slender body. He sat in a plain wooden chair and crossed his legs. "So . . ." he said, "you're having some problems. And you're here to find a way to resolve them."

Mom and Dad nodded.

Dr. Embers continued, "The good news is you're all healthy, intelligent people. My job is to help you understand the patterns that cause the difficulties so you can make the changes that will enable you to live together in harmony." I waited for him to give us the bad news, but he didn't.

"Okay, just to break the ice," he said, "I'd like each of you to describe in one word or phrase how you feel about being here today." He looked directly at me. "Rachel . . . why don't you begin."

"Me?" I said. "Why start with me?"

"Because you're the child prodigy," Charles said.

"You see!" I told Dr. Embers. "There's the problem!"

"You seem angry, Rachel," Dr. Embers said.

"I am angry!"

I expected him to say, *Can you tell me about that?* But he didn't. He just nodded and said, "Go on . . ."

But I couldn't. I mean, I didn't really know anything about Dr. Embers. I didn't know whose side he was on or how much Mom and Dad had told him. And I certainly didn't know if I could trust him. "I'm angry . . ." I hesitated for a second. "I'm angry because I don't want to be here."

He nodded again.

"But I've been told I have no choice," I continued. "I have to be here even though there's nothing wrong with me or my family . . . except for . . ."

"Except for?" Dr. Embers said, leaning slightly forward. His jacket fell open and I noticed he was wearing a silver belt buckle with an Indian design etched into it. Dad has one almost exactly like it.

"Except . . ." Dr. Embers said again, expectantly.

When I couldn't get the words out, Jessica did it for me. "Except for Charles!"

"Except for Charles," Dr. Embers repeated matter-of-factly.

"Yes," Jess continued. "He gets all the attention. He takes up all our time and energy. I'm exhausted just from living in the same house with him. It's like . . ." Jessica choked up. "It's like being slowly poisoned!"

Dr. Embers turned to Charles, who was rocking back and forth in his chair, a frozen expression on his face. "What are you feeling right now, Charles?"

"Nothing," Charles said. "Absolutely nothing."

But I didn't believe him.

We came home from our session with Dr. Embers with what he called a contract for family living. It runs for two weeks. By then I'll be on my way to music camp. I can't wait! In the contract we each agreed to try to respect one another's feelings, needs and concerns. We agreed to think before speaking. We agreed to exercise each day, if only for twenty minutes, because Dr. Embers says exercise is a good way to get rid of hostility. And we're not supposed to go to bed at night feeling angry. Even Charles signed the contract without any snide comments. Even he was too worn down to argue. When we got home, Dad taped it to the refrigerator.

The next day I signed up for Natural Helpers. I don't think I'd be a good Natural Helper if I came from a family with no problems. But I know what problems are. I know how they feel. So maybe I can help someone else feel better.

NINETEEN

Charles has new wraparound sunglasses. Dana gave them to him. I remember when she gave Jeremy Dragon a gold dove. He wore it pinned to his underwear. At least that was the rumor. I wonder if he gave it back to her when they broke up. I wonder if Charles will give back the wraparounds if he splits with Dana.

"So how about it?" Dad said to Charles. He was trying to convince him to go to Ellis Island tomorrow with his sophomore history classes. Ellis Island is the place where our family name was changed from Rybczynski to Robinson.

"I'm thinking about it," Charles said. He was wearing his sunglasses even though it was almost dark.

We were outside on our patio. It was very still, more like August than June. Dad lit a citronella candle to keep the mosquitoes away. Mom was working late at the office again. Now that her big trial is over, she says she has so much to finish up before she's sworn in as a judge she doesn't know how she'll ever get it done. I'm worried about her. A woman like Mom needs kids like Jess and me, who don't give her any trouble!

"I can't make you go," Dad said to Charles. "But it would mean a lot to me if you did."

I really felt for Dad, so I said, "I'll go."

"Me, too," Jessica added.

"There!" Charles said to Dad. "Why don't you take your devoted daughters instead of me?"

"This isn't an *instead*," Dad said. He looked at Jess and me. "For the two of you it would mean missing a day of school."

"Nothing ever happens the last week," Jess told him. "You know that."

"This isn't the last week," Dad said.

"It's the last *full* week," I reminded him. "Next week is all half days."

"And you're going to miss one of those to go to Mom's swearing-in ceremony," Dad reminded us.

"But, Dad . . ." Jessica argued, "Ellis Island is an example of *living* history. It's not something you can learn in a classroom."

Dad laughed. He knew Jess had him, and we knew he'd let us come. Then he looked over at Charles, who was picking up pebbles and letting them run through his fingers. "Charles?" he asked hopefully.

"I *told* you, I'm thinking about it!" Charles said.

I was thinking about Paul Medeiros, wondering if he'd be going with us. I hope so! After all, he's Dad's student teacher. Then I remembered this is a school trip and almost all school trips use buses for transportation. So I asked, "How will we get there?" I tried to sound casual, as if I didn't care one way or the other.

"There's a ferry from Battery Park," Dad said. "It's just a ten-minute trip, past the Statue of Liberty."

"No, I mean from *here* to New York," I said.

"Oh . . ." Dad said. "We've got a bus."

I knew it! I chose my next words carefully. "I could take the train and meet you in the city."

Charles pulled off his sunglasses and looked at me. "Don't tell me you still get carsick!"

"I don't want to discuss it with you!" I told him.

"Is she ever going to outgrow that?" Charles asked Dad.

"Of course," Dad told him. "When she gets her driver's license . . . if not before."

When I get my driver's license! That's three years from now. Mom used to tell me I'd outgrow it by ten, but I didn't. And for some reason the medicines that work for other people give me excruciating headaches. I *hate* getting carsick! It's so embarrassing, especially at my age. A few months ago Alison's mother invited us to visit her on the set of her TV series and I got sick on the drive into the city. We had to stop so I could throw up.

But Gena was very nice about it. She opened her purse, pulled out a pair of these things that looked like sweatbands and offered them to me. "I don't think I'd have survived the first few months of my pregnancy without my Sea-Bands."

When I hesitated, she said, "They're perfectly safe. You wear them above your wrists, with the little button pressing on your Nei-Kuan point. That's three fingers up from your wrist."

I thanked Gena and tucked the Sea-Bands into my purse. But I never wore them. Instead I slept all the way home and didn't get sick until I was in my own house.

Now I looked at Dad, hoping he'd say it would be fine for me to take the train. But before he had the chance, Charles started. "She wouldn't act like such a baby if you didn't treat her like one."

"Who are you to judge?" Jess asked him. She turned to me and said, "I'll take the train with you, Rachel."

I was so grateful I grabbed her hand.

Charles said, "What are you two . . . Siamese twins or something?"

"Yeah," Jess said. "You have a problem with that?"

"You see," Charles said to Dad. "It's always them against me. That's how it's been my whole life!"

"Oh, please . . ." Jess said. "You're not in second grade anymore, so why don't you stop acting like it!"

"You know, Jessica . . ." Charles began, "it could be a lot worse. I could be into drugs. I could be in trouble with the law. I could be a rapist or a serial killer . . ."

"Am I supposed to be grateful?" Jess asked.

"You're supposed to count your blessings."

"I do . . . every day . . . and you're not one of them!"

I waited for Dad to remind us of our contract for family living but Dana came along at that very moment, calling, "Helloooo . . . anybody home?"

Charles stood up and brushed off his hands. He opened the patio gate.

Dad called, "Be back by ten."

"Yeah . . . yeah . . ." Charles muttered.

After he was gone, Dad said, "I think she's good for him, don't you?" Jessica and I looked at each other but neither of us answered his question. Then Dad blew out the citronella candle, and Jess and I followed him into the house.

TWENTY

The weather broke overnight and the next morning was perfect, sunny and breezy. Jess and I were up and dressed at six. By the time Charles came into the kitchen Mom was gone, and it was just as well, because Charles looked like he'd slept in his clothes. "I have a sore throat," he said. "I think I should stay home."

Dad felt his forehead. "No fever."

"It could be Lyme disease," Charles told him. "My neck feels stiff."

I looked at him. There was an article about Lyme disease in yesterday's paper.

"Just get dressed, Charles," Dad said.

"I *am* dressed," Charles said. He was wearing his ELVIS IS DEAD T-shirt.

"Well then, have something to eat," Dad suggested.

"You're starting to sound just like Mom!" Charles said.

Dad pointed to the contract taped to the refrigerator and Charles shut up.

Dad dropped Jess and me at the train station in time to catch the 7:10 to New York, which was packed with commuters. When the train came along, we took seats across the aisle from a man carrying a canvas gym bag. As soon as the conductor collected our tickets and moved to the next car, the man, who was wearing a business suit, unzipped his bag and a small dog stuck out his head and looked around. Then the man pulled out a Dixie cup and fed ice cream to the dog from a spoon. Jess and I looked at each other and started laughing.

When we calmed down, I said, "Thanks for coming with me."

"I prefer the train," Jess said. "I always get queasy on the bus."

"I never knew that."

"Well, I don't get as sick as you, but with Charles on board . . ." She didn't have to finish her sentence. I knew what she meant.

When Jess pulled out her *Elle* magazine, I opened the book Dad had given me about Ellis Island. We read quietly for a while. Then I asked, "Do you think it's going to work with Dr. Embers?"

"It all depends on Charles," Jess said, holding her place in the magazine with her thumb. "On whether or not he wants to make the effort."

"What do you think?"

"I have no idea," Jess said. "But either way I'm not going to let him ruin my senior year!" She flipped through a few pages.

I wanted to tell her about the other night in the kitchen, when I asked Charles what he wanted from us and he couldn't answer. But I didn't.

"I'll tell you something, Rachel," Jess continued. "If he can't get along with us, that's his problem! I've got too much to look forward to, to let him get in my way." She flipped a few more pages, then tapped an ad for shampoo. "Just once I'd like to see a model in here with acne. Maybe someday they'll get real!"

When we got to the city, we followed Dad's directions and took the subway from Grand Central Station to Battery Park, which is at the southern tip of Manhattan. We were proud of ourselves for not getting lost.

Once we were there, we waited in line for tickets. Dad was lucky we went by train because by the time his bus pulled in, the lines for ferry tickets were so long we would have waited till noon.

When Charles got off the bus, I worried he'd make some rude remark about me in front of Dad's students but he didn't even glance my way. He was talking and laughing with a group of kids. I guess he'd recovered from his Lyme disease.

Paul was the last to get off the bus. I'd held my breath until then, afraid he wasn't coming after all. But when I saw him, I turned away quickly, so he wouldn't get any ideas. As Dad rounded up his students and led the way through the park down to the ferry dock, I hung back, feeling slightly out of place until Paul called, "Rachel . . . wait . . ."

I love to hear him say my name!

"Have you been to Ellis Island before?" he asked when he caught up with me.

"No, have you?"

"Once," he said, as we walked toward the ferry. "I took my grandparents for their fiftieth anniversary. They came here from Portugal right after they were married. Not exactly a romantic journey since they were both seasick the whole time."

Romantic journey! He said *romantic journey* to me!

"Victor tells me his father came over from Poland." Paul spoke as if we were actually having a conversation. It was weird to hear him call my father by his first name. I wonder what else he and Dad talk about. Do they talk about Charles? Do they talk about *me*? I tried to say something but felt like I had a mouthful of marbles.

We boarded the ferry with a large crowd—tourists from different countries speaking their own languages, other school classes, groups on outings, and families. We climbed to the upper deck and watched as two helicopters circled overhead. A group of Dad's students surrounded Paul, separating us. I looked around for Jessica but she was busy with friends.

I wandered around the deck, stopping when I heard a teacher scolding a boy, about ten. "Never mind Eric . . ." she told her class, "he's just looking for attention." When the ferry began to move, the other kids cheered but Eric sat down, clutching his stomach. Was he seasick already or just scared?

I sat next to him. He looked up at me. "I forgot my lunch," he said.

"Maybe one of your friends will share with you."

"I don't have any friends," he said. "Everyone hates me."

"That's really sad."

"Yeah, I know."

"You want my lunch?" I asked. Not that I wanted to give it to him, because I'd fixed things I really like. But I could always buy lunch if I had to, and he seemed so alone.

"What do you have?" he asked, perking up.

"Tuna with tomatoes and sprouts on rye."

"What else?"

"Oatmeal cookies, cranberry juice and a peach."

"I don't like any of that stuff," he said.

"Well then, I guess I can't help you."

"You're a geek!" he told me. "You're an ugly, stupid geek!"

"No wonder you don't have any friends!" I said, surprised at how angry I felt. Natural Helpers aren't supposed to get angry just because someone they're trying to help isn't grateful.

We stopped at the Statue of Liberty first. Eric and his class got off there. I watched from the deck as they marched off the ferry, two by two. When Eric turned and looked up at me, I waved. He stuck out his tongue. Well, at least I'd tried!

Our ferry waited at the statue while another group of school kids boarded. They were all wearing green foam Statue of Liberty crowns. As the ferry pulled out again, Dad began to recite the poem engraved at the base of the statue.

"Give me your tired, your poor,
Your huddled masses yearning to breathe free . . ."

A few kids in his class joined in, then a few more, until they were all reciting the poem together. When they finished, it was so quiet on deck I could hear the wind as it whipped my hair away from my face.

Next stop was Ellis Island. Dad reminded us to imagine ourselves as immigrants arriving by ship after a long, difficult journey. "You're tired, hungry, scared, but you've made it to the new country," Dad said. "You are about to start over in the land of opportunity!"

We entered the main building through a long portico and came into the Great Hall, which feels enormous. Probably thousands of people could fit in this room at once. The floor is made of white tile and the ceiling is so high it makes you feel tiny, even if you are the second tallest person in seventh grade.

If I were a thirteen-year-old immigrant girl coming into this vast hall, I know I'd have been scared, especially if I didn't understand a word of English, which most immigrants didn't.

Dad said we were free to look around on our own for an hour, then meet in front of the computers. Most kids went off in groups but I wandered by myself. I stopped at the first exhibit to look at the types of baggage the immigrants brought with them. There were trunks in all sizes. Some of them were made of wood, others of leather or what looked like cardboard. Some immigrants brought baskets as big as trunks. Some came with woven sacks in bright colors.

I closed my eyes and tried to imagine my grandfather as a little boy, clutching his mother's hand while his father carried their baggage into this Great Hall.

I climbed up the stairs to the Registry Room, where each immigrant was inspected for diseases and where some guard who couldn't pronounce or spell our family name, *Rybczynski*, assigned Grandpa and his parents the name *Robinson*.

On the third floor were display cases filled with

the immigrants' most important possessions—hand-embroidered clothes, candlesticks, bibles, photos, musical instruments. What would I take if I had to leave the country quickly, with just one small bag? My flute, definitely. Photos of my family and friends and of Burt and Harry. And my favorite books, the ones I read over and over again.

I checked my watch and discovered I'd been browsing for over an hour. I raced down the stairs and found Dad and his students gathered around Charles, who was seated at one of the computers. I pushed my way through the group until I was standing next to Dad.

Then I watched as Charles typed RYBCZYNSKI into the computer. In two seconds RYBCZYNSKI, STEFAN AND LEILAH popped up on the screen. I got goosebumps down my arms. These were my great-grandparents! Under their names was JOSEF, AGE FOUR. This was my grandfather! Charles moved the cursor down the screen to COUNTRY OF ORIGIN — POLAND.

Dad swallowed hard. He nodded several times, blinking back tears, and rested his hand on Charles's shoulder as Charles moved the cursor again, this time to DONOR — VICTOR (RYBCZYNSKI) ROBINSON.

Charles sat absolutely still, studying the screen. Then suddenly he jumped up and turned to face Dad. They looked at each other for a minute, but when Dad moved toward him, Charles took off, pushing everybody out of his way. He ran back into the Great Hall. Dad followed, calling, "Charles . . ." I followed Dad. Charles ran outside, under the portico and around to the left. He climbed up onto the seawall, where the immigrants' names are inscribed in bronze. For a minute I thought he was going to jump into the water. So did the tourists who were sitting nearby. You could hear a gasp go through the crowd. But instead of jumping, he spun around, arms outstretched, and began to recite.

"Give me your tired, your poor,
Your huddled masses yearning to breathe free . . ."

A guard spotted him and called, "You!"
But Charles didn't stop. His voice grew stronger.

"The wretched refuse of your teeming shore,
Send these, the homeless, tempest-tossed to me:"

The guard headed for him.
"Charles!" Dad called.
Charles looked right at him. His voice broke as he finished the poem.

"I lift my lamp beside the golden door."

Dad stood in front of the wall. "Come down now." Charles hesitated. Then he jumped. Dad caught him, wrapped an arm around his shoulders and shielded him from the crowd. Charles hid his face against Dad. I think he was crying.

I felt myself choking up and looked away, confused, because I was also angry! Angry at Charles for making himself the center of attention again. Angry at Dad for loving him so completely. Angry at myself for . . . I don't know what. I tried to find Jessica. I needed to share this with her. But Jess was nowhere in sight.

"**W**here were you when we were at the computers?" I asked her later.

"Upstairs, with my friends," Jess said. "Don't tell Dad, okay?"

"You missed . . ."

"What?"

"Seeing our family name."

"Really?" Jess said. "Well, maybe I'll go back in and have a look."

"It won't be the same."

"Of course it'll be the same. It's a computer."

"No," I said. "It wasn't just the computer."

"Then what?"

I couldn't find the words to tell her what I sensed—that something between Charles and Dad had changed forever, something I could feel but couldn't explain. So I just shook my head and said, "Never mind."

"Rachel . . ." Jess said, "you're acting very weird!"

At the end of the day, as we got off the ferry at Battery Park, I told Jessica, "I'm thinking of taking the bus home. That is, if you don't mind."

Jessica looked surprised. "Really?"

I took the Sea-Bands out of my purse, where they've been since Gena gave them to me. "I've been meaning to try these," I explained. I slipped the bands onto my wrists, then moved them three fingers up exactly the way Gena had showed me. I hoped the buttons were pressing on my Nei-Kuan points.

"Do you want me to sit next to you," Jess asked, "or can I sit with my friends?"

"You can sit with your friends."

When we boarded the bus, I took the first seat. Mom says you're less likely to get sick if you sit up front and look straight ahead, out the driver's window.

Charles seemed like his old self as he got on, talking and laughing with a group of kids. He was surprised when he saw me but he didn't say anything. He just walked by, toward the back of the bus.

When Dad saw me, he looked concerned. "Rachel, are you okay?"

"Yes," I said. "I just want to try these." And I held up my wrists, showing him the Sea-Bands.

"Good for you!" he said.

After all of Dad's students were accounted for and seated, Paul got on the bus. "Is this seat taken?" he asked, tapping the one next to mine.

I shook my head. "I don't know about you, Rachel," he said, sinking low, "but I'm zonked." Then he closed his eyes and slept most of the way home, waking only when we made a sharp turn or a sudden stop.

I can't say whether it was the Sea-Bands or the distraction of having Paul Medeiros sleeping next to me, but I made it back without getting sick!

When we got off the bus at the school parking lot, Paul yawned, stretched, adjusted his glasses and said, "There's a concert at the college tomorrow night. Would you like to go?"

Would I like to go?

"Does that look mean *yes*?" he asked.

I think I nodded.

"It's at six-thirty," he said, "so I'll have you home by nine . . . in case you were worrying."

This time I found my voice. "I wasn't worrying," I told him.

TWENTY-ONE

I was bursting! As soon as we got home, I ran over to Alison's to tell Gena the good news about the Sea-Bands. But when I got there, Leon said she was resting. "Her blood pressure's up and she's supposed to stay off her feet. Only a month to go . . ."

I told him I hope Gena feels better soon, then ran up to Alison's room. She was sprawled across her bed, her head hanging over the edge. Stephanie was there, too, sitting cross-legged on the floor, jotting something down in a notebook. As soon as they saw me, Steph closed the notebook and she and Alison looked at each other as if they knew something I didn't. But for once I didn't care. I sat on the edge of the bed and gave Maizie a few pats.

Steph could tell something was up because she said, "What?"

"Oh, nothing . . . except I'm going to a concert at the college tomorrow night . . . with Paul."

"Who's Paul?" Steph asked.

I had to be careful since I'd never even hinted how I feel about him. "You know . . . Charles's tutor."

"Wait!" Steph said, holding up her hand. "If you're going to a concert, that means you can't come to the carnival with us." The Jaycees sponsor a weekend carnival every year. Steph and I always go.

"We could go Saturday, instead," I suggested.

"Dad's taking Bruce and me to the city on Saturday," Steph said.

"I'm sorry, but I can't miss this concert."

"Are you telling us this is a date?" Alison asked.

"No, it's not a date," I said, although in my mind it definitely is. "My parents would never let me go on a date with someone nine years older."

"Why not?" Steph asked. "My mother's dating someone fifteen years *younger*."

"That's different," I said.

"Maybe to you . . . not to me."

"I don't know, Rachel," Alison said. "It sure sounds like a date."

I just smiled and kind of shrugged.

"Are you saying he already has a girlfriend?" Steph asked.

A girlfriend? I thought. For the first time I realized I know almost nothing about Paul's personal life, except that his grandparents came from Portugal. But what if he does have a girlfriend? What if she meets us at the concert? Worse yet, what if . . .

"So does he . . . or what?" Steph said.

"I don't know."

"Who cares if he does or he doesn't?" Alison told Steph. "Rachel is the one he's taking to the concert." She turned to me and asked, "What are you going to wear?"

"Wear?" I said.

She jumped off the bed and scooped up an armload of *Sassy* magazines. "You have to think about these things, Rachel," she said, dumping them in my lap.

After dinner I cornered Mom and asked if I could borrow her black dress to wear to the concert. She and Dad have no idea this is anything more than a friendly invitation. Mom said, "That dress wouldn't be appropriate, Rachel."

"But you wore it to a concert in New York . . . when you took Dad out for his birthday."

"That was different," Mom said. "That was a dress-up event."

"But, Mom . . . this is at the college!"

"I know, honey . . . but college students wear jeans, not gowns. Call Tarren . . . she'll tell you."

So I called Tarren and she said Mom was right. She also told me she'll be at the concert, with her Romantic Obstacle. "I'll look for you," she said.

I don't know how I got through the next day, our last full day of school. On the way out of math class

Jeremy Dragon said, "Hey, Macbeth . . . you going to the carnival tonight?"

"Not tonight," I told him. "Tonight . . ." I hesitated. "Maybe tomorrow night," I called. But I don't think he heard me because by then he was halfway down the hall with his friends.

I spent most of the afternoon in the tub, daydreaming about the *romantic journey* I was about to take with Paul. When I finally got dressed, I chose a long summer skirt and my favorite tank top. It's pale green and has a matching cardigan sweater. I thought about borrowing Jessica's parrot earrings but I didn't want anyone in my family, including Jess, to grow suspicious. Anyway, Jess was at work. So I wore my silver earrings, instead. My only real dilemma was whether or not to use strawberry-flavored lip gloss. I decided to go for it.

At five-thirty, when I heard the front door slam, I looked out my window and watched as Charles and Dana took off hand in hand. Only then did I come downstairs.

"Oh, there you are," Paul said, collecting his books. "I thought you'd forgotten."

Forgotten? Was he serious? "No," I said. "I just had a lot to do this afternoon." I tossed my cardigan over one shoulder the way models do in magazines.

Paul was wearing a blue denim work shirt with the sleeves rolled up. Mom and Tarren were right. The slinky black dress wouldn't have been right. I followed him out of the house, locking the door behind me. His car was parked out front. It's an old two-door Toyota, either gray or brown—it's hard to tell since I've never seen it clean. On the inside it was even worse. The upholstery was ragged. His seat was covered with an old blanket and mine was held together with duct tape.

"Slightly messy, huh?" Paul asked as we headed for the highway.

Until then I hadn't realized I'd been cleaning things up, folding papers and collecting gum wrappers and tucking them all into the side pocket of my door.

"No, it's fine. I'm just . . ." I almost said *compulsively neat* but caught myself in time and changed it to, "a natural helper."

When we stopped at a red light, Paul glanced my way and said, "I like that color on you, Rachel."

Which color? My tank top . . . my lip gloss? I didn't ask. I just said, "Thank you." Could he tell how fast my heart was beating? Did he know the palms of my hands were sweaty and I felt like either laughing or crying? I only hoped I could control myself. I stared straight ahead, grateful the drive to the college takes just fifteen minutes. "Do you by any chance know my cousin, Tarren Babcock?" I asked, trying to make small talk. "She's an education major."

"I don't think so," he said.

"She'll probably be at the concert."

"Is she a music lover like you?"

Lover! He said the word *lover* to me! I felt myself blush. "No," I said. "She's more into obstacles." I began to fan my face with my hand.

"Obstacles?" He laughed, as if I'd meant to be funny.

"Yes." I tried to laugh, too, but it came out more like a squeak.

"What kind of obstacles?"

"All kinds," I said. He seemed to think this was funnier yet. I wish I had never mentioned Tarren's name. How was I supposed to get out of this? Tell a joke, I thought. One of those jokes the dentist told me. But I couldn't remember any of the punch lines. I was totally hopeless!

"She sounds like someone I'd like to know," Paul said.

"Who?" I asked.

"Your cousin."

"Oh, I doubt it," I told him. I didn't add that he and Tarren would have absolutely nothing in common.

When we got to the college, we parked in a big field, then walked up a hill to a yellow-and-white-striped tent. There were rows of folding chairs set up inside and people were already taking seats. A girl handed us programs as we entered, and I followed Paul down the aisle to a pair of seats in the middle.

I knew I could easily be mistaken for a college student and for once I was glad. It's not just my height that makes me look older. It's my body. Mom says she was an early bloomer, too. She says in a few years my emotional maturity will catch up with my physical maturity. But I think it already has.

Outside the tent groups of students were settling on blankets on the lawn. I wished we could sit out there, too. It seemed much more romantic, even though the sun was still shining. If only the concert began at nine instead of six-thirty!

I read my program carefully. This was the last in a series performed by visiting musicians. Tonight it was the Connecticut Valley Chamber Players, with an all-Mozart program.

When the concert began, Paul closed his eyes. A lot of people close their eyes when they're listening to music. It helps them concentrate on what they are hearing. But I couldn't tell if Paul was concentrating or sleeping. Maybe he isn't getting enough sleep at night. Maybe he needs vitamins. I looked over at his hands, which were relaxed in his lap. They looked strong, manly. I imagined them touching my face, my hair. But then I began to feel very warm and had to use my program to fan myself.

The group of fifteen musicians played in different combinations for thirty-five minutes, took a short break, played for another half hour, then performed two encores. Paul applauded enthusiastically. He said, "Fantastic, aren't they?"

"Outstanding!" I agreed, even though they weren't.

Just as we were about to head back to Paul's car, I heard someone calling my name. "Ra . . . chel!" I knew it was Tarren even before I turned and saw her. She was already weaving her way through the tent to us.

"Hi . . ." she said, joining us.

"Hi," I answered. She looked very pretty. Her hair hung to her shoulders and she was wearing a low-cut sundress, showing off more than necessary.

"Well . . ." she said, giving me a nudge in the side. "Aren't you going to introduce us?"

I really didn't want to introduce Tarren to Paul. I didn't want anyone reminding him that I am just thirteen. But there was no way to get out of it, so I said, "Paul Medeiros, this is my cousin, Tarren Babcock." I spoke very fast and hoped Tarren wouldn't ask any questions.

A tall man with thinning hair came up to Tarren then, put his hand on her naked back and handed her a paper cup. "They didn't have lime spritzers," he told her. "Just plain seltzer."

"Thanks," she said, smiling up at him. That's when it hit me! This man, who looked as old as Dad, who wasn't even good-looking, at least not to me, was Tarren's Romantic Obstacle! She took a sip of seltzer, then introduced us. "Rachel, Paul . . . I'd like you to meet Professor Benjamin Byram." She said his name proudly, then gave me a meaningful smile. I'm not sure if I smiled back or not. I felt weird, knowing this man and Tarren were involved in *that* way.

Paul shook hands with Tarren's Obstacle. "I was in your class two years ago," he said. "Paul Medeiros."

"Of course," Professor Byram said. "I remember . . ." But I could tell he didn't. And so could Paul.

A small, pretty woman with lots of pale curly hair came up to the Romantic Obstacle then and linked her arm through his. "Sweetie . . ." he said, clearly surprised. "I thought you said you couldn't make it tonight."

"Well," she told him, "the meeting didn't last as long as I thought, and it was such a beautiful evening I asked the sitter to stay."

Tarren looked stricken—the way my father had the night Charles called him a wimp. "This is my wife, Francesca Hammond," the Obstacle said to all of us.

Francesca beamed at Paul. "Paul Medeiros! How good to see you. Where've you been hiding?"

"You two know each other?" the Obstacle asked his wife.

"Well, of course," Francesca said. "Paul is one of my prize students."

Tarren looked like she was about to be sick. She'd

turned a kind of grayish color, and one hand went to her throat. I don't think anyone noticed but me.

Francesca and Paul went right on talking. "I hear you've accepted a job teaching in Westport," she said.

"Yes," Paul said.

"That's wonderful! Come in next week and we'll have lunch. I want to hear all about it." Then she turned to her husband and said, "Darling, the baby-sitter . . ."

The Obstacle checked his watch and said, "Got to run. Nice to see you again, Paul. Glad to meet you, Rachel." He turned to Tarren and held out his hand to shake hers. "If I don't see you again, have a wonderful summer. It's been a pleasure having you in my class."

He had to pull back his hand because Tarren wouldn't let go. Then he and his wife walked away, arm in arm.

Tarren watched them for a minute, then burst into tears.

"What?" Paul asked.

Tarren just shook her head and tried to stifle her sobs by covering her mouth with her hand.

I patted her back.

"Don't tell me . . ." Paul said. "Another of Professor Byram's conquests."

Tarren looked at him. "Conquests?" she managed to ask.

Paul put his arm around her waist. "Come on," he said to me. "Your cousin needs some cheering up."

Tarren leaned against Paul as he led her to his car. I got in back, by myself. *She* sat up front, next to him.

We went to a diner and took a booth, where Tarren cried and Paul passed her napkins from the dispenser so she could blow her nose. When she shivered in her sundress in the air-conditioning, I handed her my sweater. She pulled it around her shoulders. Paul dropped a couple of coins into the jukebox on the wall and selected four songs, all hard rock, which totally shocked me. Slowly Tarren began to recover. She felt hungry, she said, and she and Paul smiled at each other, then ordered hamburgers and fries while I sipped a peppermint tea.

"He was never right for me," Tarren cooed to Paul over the apple pie and ice cream they shared for dessert. "I know that now."

"You were wasted on him!" Paul told her.

"It was like . . . I couldn't help myself," Tarren said to him. They spoke as if I weren't there, as if I were invisible. I hate being treated that way!

On the drive home I think they were holding hands. But I didn't care anymore. I just wanted it to be over. I just wanted to be alone in my room.

Finally we pulled up in front of my house. I leaned

forward and thanked Paul for taking me to the concert.

"My pleasure," he said.

"See you, Rachel," Tarren said as I got out of the car.

At the last minute I leaned back in through her window and said, "Give Roddy a kiss for me."

I knew she hadn't had the chance to tell Paul she was divorced, with a baby. Well, too bad!

TWENTY-TWO

I will never forgive Tarren for ruining what should have been the most romantic night of my life! She's such a fool, jumping from one Romantic Obstacle to another. I raced up to my room and closed the door, praying that Mom and Dad wouldn't ask any questions. I was halfway undressed when Mom knocked on my door. "Rachel . . ."

I didn't feel like explaining anything to her now.

When I didn't respond, she knocked again. "Rachel . . . there's someone here to see you."

Paul! He realizes he's made a major mistake. He wants me, not Tarren!

"It's a boy," Mom continued. "Jeremy something. Should I tell him you're already in bed?"

Jeremy . . . here? I began to get back into my clothes. "No!" I told Mom. "Tell him I'll be right down."

"Okay," Mom said. "But it's getting late."

Why would Jeremy Dragon come to my house on a Friday night at nine-thirty? It didn't make sense. Nothing made sense!

I had to shoo Harry out of the bathroom sink so I could splash my face with cold water. Then I fluffed out my hair, put on more strawberry lip gloss and flew down the stairs. I opened the front door but didn't see him.

"Pssst, Macbeth . . . over here."

I followed the sound of his voice to the maple tree.

"Hey," he said. He was wearing his dragon jacket. "How come you're all dressed up?"

"I just got back from a concert."

"Who was playing?"

"The Connecticut Valley Chamber Players."

He didn't act like that was unusual. He said, "You're really into music, huh?"

I nodded.

He smiled at me. "How about a walk?"

"Sure," I answered.

"Don't want to run into . . . you know . . . them."

Charles and Dana were about the last people I wanted to run into, too.

"So," he said, fishing something out of his jacket pocket. It was his token race car from Monopoly. "I meant to give this back to you right away . . . then I forgot . . . sorry."

"That's okay. Nobody's played since that night." Our hands touched as he gave me the car.

We walked around the pond. I was glad it was dark so none of the neighbors, including Stephanie and Alison, could see us. When we got to the tree where the raccoons live, Jeremy stopped walking and faced me. "Macbeth . . ." His voice was hoarse.

"What?" I think I sounded alarmed.

He leaned toward me and before I even knew what was happening, his lips were on mine.

"I've wanted to do that for a long time," he said.

"Really?"

"Yeah . . . ever since Halloween when you came to my house reciting that stupid poem. I liked the way your mouth twitched."

"It does that when I'm nervous."

"Like now?"

I touched my mouth. Was it twitching and I didn't even know? He took my hand away. "It's very kissable . . . you know?" He put his arms around me, pulled me close and kissed me again. My legs felt so weak, I thought I might fall over.

On our third try, I kissed him back. I felt a surge go through my whole body. My mind went blank for a minute. Never mind animal attraction, this was *electrical* attraction! When I came back to earth, I asked, "What does this mean?"

"Mean?" he said. He held my hand and we

started walking again. "It doesn't mean anything. It was . . . you know . . . just a couple of kisses."

No, I wanted to tell him! I don't know. This is all new to me. This is nothing like kissing Max Wilson at the seventh-grade dance. But I didn't say anything.

He walked me home. We kissed one more time in the shadows. Then he smiled and said, "See ya . . ."

Just when you think life is over, you find out it's not. Just when you think you'll never be foolish enough to fall for somebody else, it happens without any warning! I hope this doesn't mean I'm going to be like Tarren, jumping from one Obstacle to the next. I don't think it does. I don't think it means anything except life is full of surprises and they're not necessarily all bad.

TWENTY-THREE

The next morning Stephanie called. "How was the concert?"

"Boring."

"What do you mean by *boring*?"

"You know . . . the music wasn't that good and everyone there was ancient . . . over twenty, at least. I couldn't wait to get home!"

"So I guess you're glad it wasn't a date."

"Very!" I paused, lowering my voice. "I have important news but I can't tell you over the phone."

"Well, what are you waiting for? Come right over!"

"I kissed Jeremy Dragon!" I threw myself backward onto Steph's bed, falling on top of about thirty stuffed animals. "Not once," I told her, "not twice, but four times!"

Steph's mouth fell open. "Rachel . . . I'm so jealous!" I love the way Steph says exactly what she's feeling without worrying about it. "How did this happen?" she asked.

"I don't know. It was so bizarre. He came over to give me back a Monopoly piece and it just . . . well . . . happened."

"Does this mean you're going together?"

"No. It doesn't mean anything. It was just a . . . couple of kisses."

"Did you react?"

"You *must* be joking!"

"Rachel!" she squealed. "I can't believe this!"

"You think *you* can't!"

Mom was sworn in as a judge on Tuesday morning. I think Charles was disappointed when he introduced himself to the governor as Charles *Rybczynski* and the governor didn't say anything. I wonder if he's going to get tired of his new name.

Tarren wore a white suit and three-inch heels. She looked very . . . adult. She thanked me over and over for introducing her to Paul. They've been seeing each other every night. She says he's wonderful with Roddy. I don't want to hear about it. I made sure I wouldn't be sitting next to her at lunch.

Mom seems relieved now that she's the Honorable Nell Babcock Robinson, though she still doesn't know which court she'll be assigned to. I think she's also relieved Charles has a summer job working at the bakery in town. No one has said for sure what school he'll be going to next fall, but Jessica and I think there's a good chance it will be the high school, which means he'll be living at home. I'm trying to learn from Jess, who says we should stop thinking about him and just let Mom and Dad work it out with Dr. Embers. *I wish!*

Charles seems less angry since Ellis Island but I can't say he's changed. He's probably never going to change. He'll probably take pleasure in annoying me my whole life.

With Jessica it's completely different. We're always going to be close, no matter what. Still, I was upset when she said, "I heard about that program at the college."

"What program?"

"Challenge. Toad's brother told me."

"Oh." Until now I'd managed to put Challenge out of my mind. "You're not mad, are you?" I asked.

"Why would I be mad?" Jess said. "I learned long ago not to compete with you, Rachel. If I did, I'd just wind up resenting you and that wouldn't be good for either of us. Besides, no matter what happens at school you're still my *little* sister." She laughed and gave me an elbow in the ribs.

"Don't mention anything about Challenge to Mom or Dad, okay?"

"How come?"

"Because I haven't decided if I'm going to do it."

"Why wouldn't you do it?"

"I have my reasons," I told her. "So promise you won't say anything."

"You know I won't."

On the last day of school we got out at ten because the ninth graders were graduating at noon. When I passed Jeremy in the hall, he was carrying his red cap and gown.

"So, Macbeth . . . you hanging around this summer or what?"

"I'm going to music camp," I told him.

"Play a song for me, okay?"

"Sure."

"See you in September."

"I'll be back the end of August."

Some of his friends came along then, slamming into him. As they dragged him away, he looked back at me and waved. I waved, too. I can't believe I actually kissed him! And that come September, I might kiss him again.

"Nice that you and Jeremy get along so well." I spun around. It was Dana, dressed in her cap and gown. But her cap wasn't fastened yet and she had to hold it on with one hand.

"Nice that you and my brother do," I said.

I didn't want to go to the bakery after school but Alison insisted. She still has a *thing* for Charles. He was working behind the counter, wearing a white apron over his

T-shirt and jeans. "Well, well, well . . ." he said, "if it isn't the triumvirate! What brings you here?"

"Hunger," I told him.

He plucked a dog biscuit out of a jar and held it up. "These are quite savory. They appeal to all sizes and breeds."

"Woof, woof . . ." I said.

Steph and Alison tried not to laugh. They each bought a giant-size chocolate chip cookie. When Charles handed Alison her change, he said, "I'm still waiting for you, California."

"What about Dana?" I asked.

"Dana is my date *du jour*," he said, using the French expression. "But California is something else."

Alison had this ridiculous look on her face. I hope that's not how I looked when I was with Jeremy. "Come on . . ." I grabbed her by the hand and led her away. Steph followed.

"Good-bye, my lovelies," Charles called after us, giving Stephanie and Alison both a profound case of the giggles.

When we were outside, Steph bit into her cookie and said, "He just likes to tease you, Rachel!"

"Because you take everything so seriously," Alison added, breaking her cookie in half and sharing with me.

"I don't take *everything* seriously!" I told them. "Just *some* things."

On the way home I invited them to my house for

lunch. I felt safe knowing Charles was at work. Before we went inside, Alison said, "Guess what? As soon as Matthew's born, we're going to L.A."

"But you'll be back in time for school, right?" Steph asked.

"I think so," Alison said. "I hope so."

"But Alison . . . you have to be!" Steph said. "You're running for class president." As soon as she said it, she clapped her hand to her mouth. She and Alison exchanged a look. "We were going to tell you before you left for camp," Steph said.

"We were just waiting for the right time," Alison added.

"I mean, you acted like you didn't want to run," Steph said, making excuses. "You acted like you were only doing me a favor." She paused for a minute. "And Alison's so popular. She has a real chance of winning."

"We just thought the Dare to Care Candidate was too good to waste," Alison said.

I didn't know what to say! It's true I was going to tell Steph I can't run because of all my other activities. But I hadn't told her yet. And I certainly never imagined she'd find herself another candidate and give away the slogan she thought up for *me*.

"You're not mad, are you?" Alison asked.

"Let's just say I'm surprised," I told her.

"I want you to work on my campaign," Alison said. "You will, won't you?"

"If I can fit it into my schedule," I said, sounding

as snide as Charles. "I'm going to be really busy between Natural Helpers and Challenge."

"What's Challenge?" she asked.

"It's this program at the college for—"

But Steph didn't let me finish. "You're going to college?"

"No, it's for eighth and ninth graders. It's like . . ." I tried to find a way to describe it. "It's like enriched math . . . except . . ."

"It's for geniuses!" Steph said.

"We're not geniuses."

"It's for prodigies!" Alison said, trying out Charles's favorite word.

"We are *not* prodigies!"

"Even so," Alison said, sliding her arm around my waist, "I love having such a smart friend!"

A born politician! I thought.

"And you'll still work on my campaign, right?" When I didn't answer, she said, "Steph . . . tell Rachel you *want* her to work on my campaign."

"Dah!" Steph said. "Who'd want Rachel!" Then she tackled me to the ground and Alison jumped on top of us.

READ

Just as Long as We're Together

Judy Blume

A Yearling Book
Now available in all bookstores

ISBN: 0-440-40075-9 $4.50 U.S.
                                       $5.99 Canada

At the next bus stop six kids got on the bus and one of them
was the best looking boy I have ever seen in person in my
whole life. He looked almost as good as Benjamin Moore.

"Hey, Jeremy!" a group of boys called. "Back here . . ."

The boy, Jeremy, walked right by me on his way to the
back of the bus. As he did his arm brushed against my
shoulder. I turned around to get a better look at him. So did
Rachel. So did most of the girls on the bus. He had brown
hair, brown eyes, a great smile and he wore a chartreuse
colored jacket. I learned that color from my deluxe Crayola
crayon box when I was in third grade. On the back of his
jacket it said *Dragons* and under that, *1962*.

"He has a great body," Rachel whispered to me.

"Yeah," I said. "He's a real hunk." We started to laugh
and I could feel Rachel relax, until the bus pulled up to
school. Then she stiffened. But her homeroom, 7-202,
turned out to be right next to mine, 7-203.

(continued)

"Stay with me until the bell rings," she begged. "And promise that you'll meet me here, in the hall, before first class so we can compare schedules . . . okay?"

"Okay," I said. Alison was standing next to me. She kept putting her sunglasses on, then taking them off again.

"Look," I said to Rachel, "there go the Klaff twins. Kara's in your homeroom and Peter's in mine." The Klaff twins were in our sixth grade class. Their mother is our doctor. I figured Rachel would feel better knowing that Kara's in her homeroom.

"Well . . . I guess this is it," Rachel said. "I'm going to count to ten, then I'm going to go in."

TWENTY-FOUR

On Sunday morning I carefully packed my flute in its case and tossed my last-minute stuff, like my hairbrush and Walkman, into my backpack, along with *Anna Karenina*, the novel Charles quoted the night we had our private talk in the kitchen—the one that begins, "All happy families are alike . . ."

This is the first time I'm going to camp by bus with everyone else. I've always gone by train before. I put on the Sea-Bands and adjusted them. I hope they work! But what if they don't? What if I get sick and the driver won't pull over and . . . I stopped myself. I'm not going to get sick! Mom and Dad promised we'd be at the bus early enough for me to get a seat in the first row.

I walked around my room one last time, stopping to touch the box with the secret compartment. It's always hard for me to leave, even when I really want to. I'd said good-bye to Jess last night. Now that she's working at Going Places six days a week, Sunday is her only chance to sleep late. She says she expects her skin to be clear the next time she sees me. I hope she's right.

I went down to the kitchen to get a box of crackers for the road, just in case. Charles was standing at the counter, wolfing down a bowl of cold leftover pasta.

"What am I going to do without you for six weeks, Rachel?"

"Yeah . . . who'll you torture?" I asked.

"I don't know . . . it won't be easy." He swallowed a mouthful, then puckered up. "Kiss your big brother good-bye?"

"I sincerely hope you're kidding."

"Would I kid you, little sister?"

"You would if you could."

"I'll be counting the days till we're together again."

"Me, too," I said. "I hope they go really slowly."

"Rachel, is this possible . . . you're developing a sense of humor?"

"Anything's possible!" I told him. Then I walked out the door, laughing to myself.